LOVE
and the
EPIDEMIC

LOVE
and the
EPIDEMIC

a novel

by

BRUCE K BECK

AUDACITY BOOKS
WE DARE TO TELL THE TRUTH
New York

Also by Bruce K Beck:

You're Sure to Fall in Love (Audacity Books, 2017)

Produce: A Fruit and Vegetable Lovers' Guide (Friendly Press, 1984)

The Official Fulton Fish Market Cookbook (E P Dutton, 1989)

ISBN: 978-0-9991182-6-9

This is a first edition from Audacity Books. Visit us on the web at www.audacitybooks.com For information about rights or purchases, please email us at info@audacitybooks.com.

For the fallen,
those I love, and those I never got to love.

Prologue

I swear to you, I never wanted to write about the AIDS Epidemic. I always thought, no, it is too painful, and others have gone there, and what street-cred do I have as a serum-negative gay man? What could I possibly add to the literature? What do I know? What do I know that no one else knows? What do I know that anyone else would like to know, to share, to remember? Beats the hell out of me. And yet, here I am: typing away.

Let me start with a confession. Perhaps you will understand my character better if I share my reactions to another disaster: I never took any photos of Ground Zero after 9/11. It seemed almost disrespectful, that it was somehow none of my business. Heading down there with a camera would have felt like an intrusion on the solemn gravity of the loss. I was something of a neighbor, having written *THE OFFICIAL FULTON FISH MARKET COOKBOOK*. My Market tours were canceled, of course. There was one scheduled for the following morning. Fulton was directly opposite World Trade on the narrow downtown street grid. Chinatown was as close as I got in those first months after the disaster, and seeing its vibrancy all but masked by the gray dust of ruin was enough to send me right back uptown.

Surfacing from the subway the first time I went to work on West 23rd Street after the towers came down, I had to force myself to stop and look down Sixth Avenue. And there, sure enough, where the towers had stood all those years, was fucking *nothing*! Now, I go to that neighborhood every weekend, and while I rarely take the F train these days, I never fail to gaze down the avenue at the new Freedom Tower and remember how different the world seemed not so many years ago.

The Epidemic feels very much the same to me. Call me a coward, if you wish. I do. But the act of writing this book has left me richly invested in the pain, the loss, the grief, the outrage. I set out to tell a story that I hope will honor the victims, and perhaps even make some sense of it, in one way or another. For me, for you, for. . .who knows?

Every book tells its author what structure it needs, I think. Those who liked *YOU'RE SURE TO FALL IN LOVE* will notice that this time, many of my characters have a story to tell. And I have tried to get out of their way and just let them tell it. I could try to dazzle you with my skill at weaving bits of story together to produce a suspenseful whole. But, out of respect, I have often just given my characters an open mic. So if Volume II reads more like a collection of short stories than Volume I did, now you know why. And, Dear Reader, I hope you will approve. The writing experience has been joyous and deeply moving, as I hope the reading will be for you.

New York City
March 2018

Chapter One

Scooter was particularly insistent that morning. He twirled and made soft growly noises that gradually grew louder as no one noticed that he wanted *very* much to go outside. Bobby was still sound asleep, but the performance was enough to get my attention. I sleepily dragged myself out of bed and opened the garden door for poor Scooter. I felt a little blast of winter cold on my naked body. It was refreshing. Therapeutic even. *Shit! Ten o'clock already!* I thought.

And then all Hell broke loose. Scooter let out a full-throated howl that showed no signs of stopping. I ran to the window and looked out. And there, in the middle of the garden, was a huge orange cat. Or rather, the *body* of a huge orange cat, now flattened and motionless on the slate tiles. I threw on a robe and slippers and dashed out to coax Scooter back into the apartment. It took some doing to break his obsession with the intruder, but before long I got him back in and mercifully quiet.

Bobby was roused by the commotion, of course. "You're not going to believe what's in our garden," I said.

"You're being mysterious," he said.

"No, really. You have to look."

Bobby went to the window and peered out. "Jesus Christ!" he said. "What a way to start the new year."

It seemed so unlikely. Cats are so, well, capable. I would almost have been less surprised to see a New Year's Eve reveler of the two-legged variety flattened in our garden. That had logic on its side. I dispensed with analysis and threw on some clothes. It was only one short hallway to the lobby, where the doorman would certainly have a handle on this.

"Tom, there's a dead cat in the garden," I said quietly.

"Ouch! Poor Mr. Segal in 14F. He's frantically looking all over the building for his cat. He should check in here again pretty soon. Can I send him to your apartment?" Tom asked.

"Of course," I answered, and headed back. Bobby was in the kitchen putting the kettle on for coffee. "The owner should be here any minute to collect the body," I warned. "Segal, in 14F."

"I thought cats survived falls like that. Fourteen floors shouldn't be such a challenge. Maybe it was sick. Or old. Let's not go there." Bobby finished the brewing, and we sipped our coffee in silence. He thought to go to the linen closet and pull out an old towel, to use as a shroud. And then came the horrible knock on our door. I grabbed Scooter and quieted him while Bobby went to the door and admitted our neighbor, who was visibly shaken and choking back sobs. Bobby led him to the bedroom and out to the garden. Scooter and I followed as far as the garden door. Segal identified the body and began to sob in earnest.

Bobby handed him the towel to wrap the corpse in. "Keep it," Bobby said. And then Segal managed a quiet thank-you before scooping up the body and heading back to his apartment to grieve. "I wish we hadn't invited people over this afternoon," Bobby said.

"Tell me," I said. We had twelve guests coming for a New Year's Day buffet. Roast fresh ham, collards, and Hoppin' John. I had made a green tomato chow-chow that fall: When the first frost threatens, farmers and gardeners alike pull the green fruit from the vines and sell it off to home canners and other crazies, like me, who lovingly convert it into a relish that brings a touch of summer to the table even in the dead of winter. I was proud to be able to offer it. Cornbread, and a real banana pudding to round out the meal. Everything guaranteed to bring health and prosperity for the new year. "Looks like we're going to need all the good luck we can gather this year," I said.

"Lucky we're neither of us superstitious. Are we?" Bobby asked.

"Of course not." I answered, without much conviction. So, there I was, nervous, with a nervous dog, a nervous husband, a heart-broken neighbor, and about five hours to pull things together to receive twelve friends I hoped would feel relaxed and warmly welcome. I had done much of the cooking the day before, so I even considered going back to bed for an hour, to try to restart our day.

But reason won out, and Bobby and I began to lay out the buffet things and get organized. I stopped to make two grilled cheese sandwiches (what is more comforting?). Good bread, good cheese, and good butter would have been enough, of course, but I couldn't resist adding a few very thin slices of plum tomato and a slice of leftover cooked bacon to each sandwich. We had a bite of lunch and a stiff vodka. They both helped.

As I figured out the design for our buffet, I thought to myself, *Shit! Another New Year's Day. How is that even possible? Should I be taking inventory or something? Almost ten years*, I reflected, *since our glorious summer in Provincetown. Where did those years go? Can I account for them? What have I done? What have I learned? Where am I now?*

You wrote a book, I reminded myself. And so I did. And a few magazine articles. And hundreds of teaching recipes. *You show up for work, even early sometimes, and you give it your all. Well, at least you do a professional job at all times. People like you. They take one of your classes and come back for more.*

I looked over at Bobby, who was busy dusting and vacuuming, fluffing cushions and checking tabletops for smudges. I loved watching him when he was absorbed and didn't see my stare. It was most often when he was working at the piano, but he focused intently on even the more mundane tasks. I thought how much I still adored Bobby after our ten years together, and how much I loved my life.

Wouldn't you know I'd choose a Southern theme for our holiday feast! What the hell was I doing there? Back there! What did the South have to offer me? As I returned to the kitchen to finish up the food prep, I felt some twinges going through my body. I don't have flashbacks, or at least not in the psychotic sense, I hope. But now and then I am visited by shades of childhood. No, not shades, sparks! Little explosions of light like jagged knife blades. Like the aura that signals a migraine that will take complete control of my body unless I fend it off. With drugs, mostly. And, of course, alcohol is a powerful one—sometimes for good and sometimes for ill.

Whenever I see screen depictions of war, the hapless victims who can't get out of the way of the bombs or bullets always make me think, *Yeah, that's about right. That's how childhood felt. Sometimes I could see it coming, and sometimes not. But, either way. . . .* And I was one of the lucky ones! My parents didn't beat me, or starve me, or deprive me. I had it good, by most standards. But I felt desperately alone, and uncertain if I could ever wake up from the nightmare.

Does everyone feel the white heat of humiliation from childhood? No one ever called me a nigger, or a wop, or a kike, or a Chink, or a Jap, or even a faggot, for that matter. Well, not back then. But I felt it. I felt a circle of fresh young bodies and sweet faces around me, taunting me. A chorus assembled solely for the purpose of ridicule. It's the betrayal, I think. It's the moment when a friend becomes a tormentor. It's not even so much about the importance of the secrets revealed as it is about confidence breached. It's the deliberate cruelty (isn't that what Tennessee Williams called it?).

Look, I know I was not the Jewish kid whose best friend joined the Hitler Youth and turned him in. I know I didn't have dinner one night with our Serbian next-door neighbors, only to see them take part in the roundup of Croatians the next day. I get it. I can't equate the experiences. And perhaps that's part of why I've spent so many years sweeping the pain under the carpet. Except, of course, inevitably—it's still there! It doesn't go away on its own any more than the dirt under the rug does.

As I look back on the 1980s, I'm amazed by all the dinners I staged. We must have had a dinner party nearly every week. Nothing elaborate, usually, just a couple of friends over for drinks and a bite. Farther into the decade, I grew busier and less willing to commit the time to these little events. But in the mid-80s, we were still host central. It's how we socialized. And how we did business, sometimes, too. Restaurants were for occasions, out-of-town guests, and those now-and-then pre- or post-theater get-togethers. But the meat-and-potatoes of it was people entertaining at home. And we drank. A lot.

I loved it. I came from a household where there was absolutely no entertaining. Out-of-town family were fed, of course, and Mother had to host her garden club about twice a year. That meant instant coffee served from one of those glass carafes with the gold trim sitting on a brass wire stand with a warming-candle (and to this day I'm awed by them when I see them at the flea market. And I do). And something to eat, of course. But I have no memory of what that was, exactly. I know my mother never crafted a tea sandwich in my presence. Or anything else of the sort. I don't know what she served.

I knew something was missing. And when I finally grew up—perhaps—enough to be on my own, I noticed right away that gay boys entertained! I learned later that the gay entertaining movement—like so many other social movements—got off to a bumpy start: the boys did not know how to cook. And so they did the same thing that the girls did— who also didn't know how to cook: they served tuna noodle casserole. To the point that it became known as Fairy Pudding.

One of our guests, Nigel, came to me that year and suggested we collaborate on a cookbook called **Beyond Fairy Pudding**. I always thought it a good idea. And like so many other good ideas, it never bore fruit. But I felt blessed to be coming of age in a universe where boys *did* know how to cook. And I was one of them. And I rejoiced in it. And the care of my guests felt like a sacred trust that I assumed freely and totally.

I'm sure if I had a head count—which I do not—I could prove that at least as many women dined at our table that year as men. But my story is about 1986, and it is not only about love, but also about the epidemic. And while love sends my heart in several directions, the epidemic focuses me—laser-like—on those boys, those exquisite young men who passed through my life, through my orbit, through my consciousness, and sometimes through my bed, and then didn't survive the decade.

That New Year's Day, I sucked up my bitterness about the past, reburied it in its old plot, and got on with the business of life. When four o'clock arrived, Bobby and I were feeling festive, indeed. And as soon as a few guests had arrived, Scooter, too, seemed ready to party. Our neighbor Janet arrived first, just for a quick drink on her way to another engagement. Also stopping by for a bit of holiday cheer was our neighbor Diana with her boyfriend Chris. Diana is the one that Bobby used to refer to as the QEII, because she was English and very large. And my fellow late-night dog-walker Paula arrived with her husband James. They, too, were off to another dinner party after sharing a drink and a nibble with us.

Our dinner guests were Bobby's old friend Geoffrey, whom he always liked to include (I was less enthusiastic about Geoff, but more on that later); an Oscar-winning actress and her Oscar-nominated husband; a good friend of Bobby's—and frequent reciprocal dinner host—who was bringing her two college student children, a boy and a girl, home on holiday recess, who were both charming and maybe a bit star-struck; two new friends from Brazil, who were quite beautiful—as all Brazilians are, of course; Nigel, mentioned before, and his boyfriend, Steve; and two of the hottest men I've ever clapped eyes on—the dancer/choreographer Johnny Barnett and his dancer/singer mate Josh Walker.

I'll tell you more about Johnny and Josh later, especially Josh, but for now, it's enough to say that they were both very tall, very black, very handsome, and very engaging. And Johnny choreographed a new dance routine that evening for Scooter, who was just as beguiled by the two as were the rest of us. It was a good mix. It was a fabulous dinner, if I do say so myself. And it was all over by ten o'clock. I think everyone was relieved that the party season ended on an up-beat and early note. I know we were. Re-entry into normal life is always difficult, but even worse when lost sleep and a hangover are factors.

Bobby and I started the cleanup and decided to see how much we could accomplish in an hour, which was considerable. I left the glassware for morning, and Bobby would have to run the vacuum, of course, but other than that, we were in good shape. Scooter got a decent walk—if not the extra-long version—and then it was off to bed and a little television. "Thanks for all your help today," I said.

"Thank *you*, for a lovely dinner," Bobby said.

"I love you, Darling," I said.

"I love you more."

"Happy New Year," I said.

"And to you, Sunshine."

It felt like a successful evening, and the perfect start for a successful new year. And yet, as my head hit the pillow, I felt a little jolt of unease just behind my eyes. Visions of dead cats danced in my head. Quite different from sugarplums. Mercifully, it didn't last long. That time.

Chapter Two

The next week, when I got home from teaching an evening class, Bobby said, "I got a call from Richie, Jan's friend."

"Oh, right. How are they?" I asked. I always liked Richie Sullivan, ever since he greeted us at the front door of the Pilgrim House when we arrived to work for Jan Cooper in Provincetown, in the summer of 1976.

"Not so good, as it happens. Ritchie's fine, actually. But Jan's in bad shape."

"How so?" I asked.

"Well, he's sick, for one thing. It doesn't look good. And he's broke."

"But the hotel," I said. "Wasn't that supposed to float his retirement?"

"I guess the numbers didn't add up, because he lost the hotel and now he owes back rent on his apartment uptown."

"Shit!" was about all I could manage.

"Ritchie is organizing a benefit concert. It's going to be in two weeks. Of course, I told him I would be happy to help. I already called Mary, and she can do it. And I left a message for Dorothy. It's going to be a Sunday night, so there shouldn't be any big availability problems, even for people who are working. I have to get a phone number for the

Knickerbocker boys; that shouldn't be too difficult. Judy knows them. And Mary's going to call Sylvia."

I felt worthless, and said so. "Don't be silly, Sunshine. It's not your problem. But you can run a follow-spot. Does that make you feel more worthwhile?"

"Yes, it does. Thank you," I said. It was hard to believe that nearly a decade had passed since we were all together in P'town. Well, not exactly all together *at once*. The various ladies and the boys had played the guest spot—the late show—for a few weeks at a time, while Bobby and I were there for the whole bloody summer.

That means that Bobby played Jan's show eighty times, at least, plus Mary's show for another twenty performances or so. And whether I was working the early show—Bunny Babbit's drag/variety show—plus Jan's show, or Jan's show plus the late show, I must have served many thousands of drinks. The customers are now all a blur, but I'll bet I remember some of those acts better than the creators would.

Backstage, after the tech rehearsal, I was delighted to run into my old friend Randy, one of Jan's dancers that summer.

"Why, Nolie! Will wonders never cease!" he said.

"Randy, I'm so glad to see you!" I said. "You look. . .*very* thin."

"Hush, Child. Enough said."

"Where is. . ."

"In the hospital, actually. He was having a *really* bad day," Randy said.

"What. . .what's going on?"

"Business as usual, I'm afraid."

"I didn't know," I said.

"We haven't really told *anybody*. But there's no hiding it anymore."

"Is there *anything* I can do?" I asked, pathetically.

"You could smile more," Randy said. "Smile, Magnolia!" he said, and the memories of his Cap'n Andy impression filled me with sweetness—for the innocence of time past. But I also shuddered with dread—for what was to come.

"What will you do?" I asked, lamely.

"We'll play it one day at a time," Randy said. "We both have big ol' Southern families that we hoped to avoid forever. My mama, his mama—there are people who would take us in. There are possibilities. I'd rather just die than be separated from him. But my choices are not always my own these days. Did you know that we've been lovers since high school?"

"No, but I knew it was a while," I said.

"After our senior prom, we both took our dates home, and then met in the town park and kissed so long that our lips were bruised. I never could get enough of his mouth. We decided then and there to break out of that town. And we did! We moved to Atlanta. And then we moved to New York. And the rest is history."

"And a charming history it is," I offered.

"Let me go," Randy said. "I've got to go to work!" And so he did. I didn't get to run a follow-spot, after all. It was a union house, and a full complement of tech people had to be employed. But I suggested gel colors and specific cues, since I knew all the performers. So I got my two cents' worth in anyway.

The show went very smoothly. When Randy came on, the spot-operator caressed him with Surprise Pink, and the lighting, combined with stage makeup and stage energy, made him look young and dewy fresh. The picture of health. I wondered how much longer he could pull that off.

It really was a delightful show, everyone giving it their all. At the end, when Jan was helped onstage by his two long-time dancers to take a bow and say thank you, the entire audience leapt to their feet, of course. We gave him the warmest possible send-off, for this was obviously going to be his last stage appearance. The proceeds from the show did maybe cover his debts, more or less, leaving Jan to die in peace, the following year.

I went to visit Randy a few days after the show. He was home alone. His boyfriend was still in the hospital. Randy seemed a bit at loose ends, but otherwise fairly together. He had pulled on an old sweater and some well-worn jeans. It was a *comfortable* meeting. The radiator in the living room hissed and clanked, and the room seemed much too warm. I would learn to accept that as normal, in the years to come.

Randy made coffee. I brought some croissants from my new favorite bakery. We sat at the little table at his kitchen window. It was an old West-Side apartment. Small, but with a kitchen that actually had a window. So you *know* it was an old building. The coffee was good—from Zabar's, most likely—and Randy heated some milk in a saucepan on the stove. I don't mind that little skin that forms on the surface of the milk when it's heated. A little texture in my coffee does me no harm.

As the diffused sunlight from the kitchen window illuminated Randy's dear face—with its traces of ancient acne and evidence of life lived, some subtle and some not so subtle—I looked deeply into his eyes and decided that they were blue/green. Yes. That was my assessment, for the record. Randy's left hand was resting on the table, and I placed my right hand on top of it. We sat. We sipped. We munched. And I held Randy's hand as long as I could justify the gesture. We had never actually held hands before, as far as I remember, and yet it seemed perfectly natural to me that two old friends should sit, and hold hands, and be silent.

"How many more seasons did you do with Jan?" I asked, after Randy got up to pour us more coffee.

"Two," Randy said. " '77 and '78. It's really only a few years ago, and yet it seems like another life."

"Could I ask," I said, with trepidation, "about Bunny?"

"His Fabulousness, Bunny Babbit, bit the dust two years ago," Randy said.

"No one told us," I said, "and yet I had a sense of it, or at least I was very much afraid to ask about him."

"He worked right up until the summer before. And then he just couldn't do it anymore. Jan has friends who asked us to come up and clear out Bunny's apartment. He had a picture of the two of you on his night-table."

"A picture of Bobby and me?" I asked.

"No, Nolie, a picture of *Bunny* and you. Taken at the club one night that summer."

"I had no idea."

"Well you must have been there, Nolie, 'cause it's your mug, right next to his. The queen and her page-boy," Randy said. "Actually, I think I can find it. And you should have it."

"No, no. That's not fair," I said. "It's your photo. You should keep it."

"Nolie, I don't have much use for souvenirs these days. I want you to have it."

"Of course," I acquiesced.

Randy went to his bedroom and rummaged around a bit. He called me in to see the small trunk he found under the bed with memorabilia from P'town. Menus, flyers, photos, reviews and other clippings, props from Jan's shows. They even *smelled* like summer on the Cape. And sure enough, about half-way into the pile, he found the photo of Bunny and me. It was in a handsome little frame with faux-tortoiseshell trim.

I gasped in shock at the young face that stared back at me. Quite different, I thought, from the face that met my gaze in the mirror these days. My old friend and mentor, however, looked precisely as I remembered him—sassy, stern, formidable, defiant, courageous. And yet just behind the in-your-face outrageousness, Bunny had a core of sweetness that I knew about, of course, but that I thought he kept well hidden. And yet, in that photo, there it was for all to see.

"He had this on his nightstand?" I asked.

"Yup."

"But, why?" I asked.

"Probably because he liked the way he looked in it. Why do you think, Nolie? Bunny was in love with you."

"Shut up!" I said. "Randy, he never. . . ."

"Don't tell me you didn't know."

"I didn't."

"Well, then the foolish child I've been so fond of all these years turns out to be stupid, too."

"Oh, Randy," I said, "Bunny never gave me the slightest indication that he wanted anything more than friendship."

"So, you think he should have made a pass at Bobby's husband and upset the whole apple cart? Grow up, Nolie. In the real world, we don't always get what we want. And so, we settle," Randy said.

"Not you, Randy," I said. "You don't just settle."

"Not in my *relationship*. I found my perfect partner when we were still children. We're blessed. But look at career. Do you think I grew up dreaming of working with Jan Cooper? I love Jan, don't get me wrong, but his drag show was not what I had in mind when I spent all those years in dance class. I wanted to dance for Balanchine."

"You certainly have the butt for it," I said.

"Damn straight!" Randy said, "Excuse the word. Anyway, take the fucking picture. It's yours. Here's a bag, for mercy's sake. You don't make it easy."

📖

Life, what was left of it, was not easy for Randy and his partner. Boyfriend got out of the hospital the next day, and the two of them had a few months of relatively normal life before the *disease*

17

du jour became too much for them to deal with on their own. And, of course, they were neither of them really able to work, so the cost of maintaining a Manhattan apartment—even a modest one—also became too much for them to deal with on their own. City and state programs helped. At least all of their meds were covered automatically. I helped them find a rent assistance program.

With deep despair and a sense of defeat, Randy accepted his mother's invitation to take them in. At least they would be together. Randy told me that that was the only way he would consider it: "Two boys or no dice." And Mama came through. So many families didn't. I knew they would never find happiness in their old hometown, but happiness seemed beside the point by then.

I went by the apartment, now nearly bare, to see them off. Anything of value—and some household items of questionable value—had been donated to a new AIDS charity. And the rest went out in the trash. They had sold the car by then. When they had turned the key for the last time in the door-lock of their little love-nest of twelve years, they walked down to the street with two small suitcases each and waited for a taxi to take them to the train station.

The good-byes were quick. A taxi pulled up right away. I was able to manage a quick hug and a quick kiss with each of them, and they were on their way. The boys were resigned. I, on the other hand, was filled with fresh outrage and also fresh pity—for myself—because I knew I would never see them again. It was very hard for me to let them go. But, as Randy had said, my choices were not always my own those days.

Chapter Three

Bobby got a phone call in mid-January, the week before the benefit concert, from a man he had known for at least ten years, a guy who made heaps of money in some sort of business or other. Legal? Who knows? But the man had particular show-business favorites, like Mary and Bobby, and he was pleasant enough and enjoyed spending his money.

Leonard Gravina was his name, and he called to invite us to his villa in St. Thomas and a few weeks cruising around the Caribbean on his yacht. Bobby promised to check with me and get right back to him. "He wants to fly us down on his jet, from Teterboro, on February first. A week in St. Thomas, and then, the boat, for, well, maybe the rest of the month, at the pleasure of his guests. And, by the way, his guests are mostly us and Simon Hayley and his boyfriend."

I had never met Simon Hayley, but I was slightly awed by his fame as a performer/songwriter and his legendary marriage to—no, don't get me started on gossip. I'll only just say that he was one of the hottest things out of Australia since "Waltzing Matilda," and I had no problem with the idea of spending time with him. "I don't know if we can do this, Sunshine," Bobby said, "but I thought it would be a very nice birthday gift for you, if you want it."

"Well, yes, but, shit! How could either of us disappear for a month?"

"I had an idea," Bobby said. "I can clear the first week in February. If you can, too, then we could maybe go down for the first week, in St. Thomas, and then fly home together. I think we might just be able to scrape together the fare for two one-ways."

"Give me a minute to check my calendar," I said. I checked, made a phone call, and almost within the span of the promised minute, I agreed. Bobby phoned Leonard, who accepted our limited participation in the holiday. And it was all arranged. All in that afternoon. Isn't life full of surprises?

We gathered at Teterboro—Bobby and I, Simon and his friend Jeremy, Leonard and his girlfriend Marti, the pilot, copilot, and flight attendant. I had never been in a Learjet before, so I didn't know what to expect. I was actually quite nervous, afraid that I would hate it. I went for the vodka as soon as possible. But it turned out to be a flight, just a flight, like any other, except that the plane was smaller, there were only six passengers, and the flight attendant was determined to make us as comfortable as possible.

It was also my first trip to the Caribbean, so I had no idea what to expect from St. Thomas. I didn't know, then, how different each island is, how different the flavor of each tropical paradise. St. Thomas, in those days, was still fairly quaint and charming. I liked the fact that it was hilly and not all beaches and palm trees. The villa was nestled into the side of a small mountain, just above town. It was entirely private and secluded, and yet just minutes from everything in downtown Charlotte Amalie.

Simon's friend Jeremy was a nice-looking guy, maybe thirty, about my height, with dark hair and pale skin. Jeremy and I were the two who worried about sunburn the whole week, while the others didn't give it a thought. The other thing that Jeremy and I had in common, besides our fragile skin, was that we both had a keen sense of not wanting to be seen as boy-toys for our older mates. I should have aged out of the category by then—thirty-six is hardly jail-bait—but these things are relative. Bobby would always be twenty years senior, and I would always look a bit light-weight to some observers. I sensed that Jeremy was dealing with the same issue, and it made me like him all the more. And the fact that he had an exceptionally cute butt did no harm.

It was a lovely week. We slept late, had breakfast by the pool, and spent our afternoons in leisurely pursuits—sunbathing for Bobby and Simon, and exploring the town for Jeremy and me. The two of us walked, and shopped, and haggled for trinkets. Jeremy was a delightful fellow explorer. He enjoyed the fish market almost as much as I did. And we laughed ourselves silly at the thought of what we could do with one of those big, prickly chayotes in the produce stands.

Our second afternoon together, as we headed back to the villa, Jeremy asked me, "Do you and Bobby have sex with other men?"

"We used to," I answered, "together. But nowadays, it's just too risky. And you?"

"Yes, that's pretty much the story. Do you miss it?"

"Well," I said. "I'm busy with work these days. But if you really want the truth, of course I miss the sex! I want it all."

"So do I," Jeremy said. "Simon is the most delightful man I could have hoped to meet. I intend to spend the rest of my life with him. But I miss. . . ."

There was a little space just off the path, just below the entrance to the villa. It was just big enough for a banana tree and the two of us. I took Jeremy's arm, and we disappeared, I hoped, behind the big green fronds that were leaning toward the path. I think I kissed Jeremy first, but it felt mutual.

We kissed. We kissed some more. We both knew we couldn't make love, however much we might have wanted it—that would be disloyal. And we couldn't even have an old-fashioned toss on a proper bed—the logistics were just too impractical. So, we did the next best thing: We stood behind the banana tree and got each other off. In unison, I might add. It was messy, but such fun that we both started to laugh as we tried to figure out where to find a source of water to douse ourselves and create the illusion of uniform wetness. Like, maybe, we had taken a dip in the ocean, or something. There was an irrigation hose nearby, conveniently. We pulled off the illusion, I think.

Jeremy and I took further dips into wetness, together, that week. Each afternoon, on our way back up from town to the villa. And once or twice in the house itself, in back hallways. But we were both young enough that we still had sufficient reserves of romantic energy for the important relationships in our very separate lives. What Jeremy and I did together physically meant nothing, and yet I also knew that I had fallen in love with him. And maybe even—a little—he with me. But it was a love that we could file away in a tender, remote place in the heart where it would never even smolder, much less burst into flame.

Leonard and his girlfriend Marti threw a birthday party for me, complete with big spiny lobsters doused with rum and set ablaze. It was great fun, and, I'll always remember the mango mousse with fresh berries that capped our feast. Leonard and Marti were perfect hosts: They offered their guests every comfort and luxury with no rules or expectations. Well, *almost* no expectations. The kinds of guests who get invited back always show up on time for cocktails and dinner and make it a point to be charming without being too *on.* That's how to sing for your supper. Bobby had the guest gene. Simon, too. Jeremy and I, sensing that our DNA was lacking, were trying to learn how to do it. And we both had skilled teachers.

Wednesday evening, Leonard and Marti had to go into town to see some friends, so the staff served dinner to the four of us guests. It was fun being on our own—easier, more relaxed. Simon, in particular, was much more engaging than I remembered from the previous evenings. I decided that he was really quite handsome without his practiced, professional smile.

Simon knew, of course, that Bobby often worked with Mary, and he said, "You know, I heard Mary sing at a club in Los Angeles in the early '70s. The audience was a little rowdy, and I thought, 'Quiet, please!' And that's why I wrote that song. I'm writing a big show—did I tell you? There's a part for Mary in it. She'll be great. Maybe next year."

"What's it like, growing up in Australia?" I asked. "I've never been there, and I don't have any sense of it." I was feeling more relaxed, too, and more interested in getting to know this exotic celebrity.

"Imagine you're in a small town in Texas. Only instead of Mexicans on the wrong side of the tracks, there are Aboriginals. I couldn't wait to get out. But growing up gay anywhere is tough, of course, so I'm not so sure I had it any worse than most. I have some nice memories, too."

"Please share one," I urged him.

"Poor Simon!" Bobby said. "Once my hubby senses a story, no one gets off the hook." I hadn't realized until that moment that I had begun to ask questions, and really listen to the answers. And listening is a very good thing indeed, I'm sure.

"Oh, that's fine," Simon said. "I'm happy to share. Do you want a family story, or something about sex?"

"Sex, please," I answered immediately. "Or love. Or both."

"Now you're onto something," he said. "They make each other better. Poor Jeremy has heard this story before. Feel free to nap, Darling."

"Whatever it is, I'm sure I'll love hearing it again," Jeremy assured him.

"That's my boy!" Simon said. He smiled, and I thought how winning he was, much more so than when he was onstage and all puffed up with performance energy and camp.

"When I was nineteen and had just moved to Sydney," Simon began, "I met a guy at a bar one night. His name was Gerald. He was about my age, and a hot little thing. But I wasn't interested in *boys*. I wanted to meet *men*, who had some experience under their belts, and could help me learn what life's all about. But Gerald was interested in me, and he really was very nice, and very sexy, and I ended up going home with him.

"Gerald was living in a depressing furnished room, not so different from mine. But when we kissed and fell into his lumpy old bed together, the tattiness of the room seemed to disappear. All I could see was Gerald with his pretty mouth and his slender young body. We embraced for hours. All I knew about before him was quickies. And now I was somewhere else entirely. "Could this be *making love*?' I wondered. It was, actually. It was the first time I ever made love to a man—well, a manchild, really. I was euphoric. We drifted off to sleep.

"The next morning I woke to the sound of Gerald making coffee on his little gas burner. The 20¢ coin made a ka-ching sound as it dropped into the meter. I was familiar with that. And the little blue flame that sprang up was so cheery that it took the edge off the dreariness of our surroundings. But more than that, I realized that Gerald was still just as cute as he was the night before. Cuter, really. Tousled hair suited him. And he had the same inviting smile and the same delicious body as the night before.

"Gerald finished making our coffee and brought it over to the bed. It was nice, but all I really wanted was Gerald. We spent our whole Sunday morning in bed, giggling and kissing and rolling around into new configurations. They were all good. That afternoon, Gerald said, 'Why don't we take a room together? We could get something a little larger and still save some dollars.'

"I was ready to say yes on the spot, but instead I said, 'Thanks, Gerald. It sounds like a good idea. But give me a minute to think about it.' Well, I did think about it, for maybe an hour. And by the time I left Gerald's flat that night, we had made our plans. We moved in together later in the week. There was an endless stream of homeless young people coming to town, so landladies weren't too concerned about being stuck with a vacancy. We just pulled up stakes on short notice and headed into our new adventure.

"The new room that Gerald found was indeed a little larger, and a little more cheerful than before. But all I cared about was that Gerald was in it. We both took stupid jobs, lost them, and found new stupid jobs. It didn't exactly feel like progress, but it certainly was fun! I don't know precisely how long we lived there. I know we celebrated my twentieth birthday in that silly flat. Gerald bought me a watch and told me maybe it would help me get to work on time. Not bloody likely. But I still have that watch. Somewhere.

"In the months that followed, I began to detect a little chill in the atmosphere. Or was it my imagination? And then one evening after I got home from work, Gerald told me, very quietly, that he was no longer in love with me, and that he had fallen in love with another guy, one of his mates from work. I was horrified, of course, but I said nothing for the next five minutes. And then I managed an almost-smile as I asked, 'Will you move out, or shall I?' And that was it.

"I never told Gerald that my heart was broken. I never really spoke to him again, beyond the necessities of breaking up our domestic arrangement. I just cut it off. No tears. Well, not then. I didn't really think that people could die of a broken heart, but I wouldn't have been too surprised if I had. But when I didn't, I started to take better care of myself. That year I got my first job singing in a nightclub, and then I started writing my own songs. And I never looked back, except to thank Gerald— mentally, that is, I never saw him again—for pushing me out of the nest. I dropped the past, *and* I never fell in love again—until this one came along." He indicated Jeremy, who, true to his word, had seemed to enjoy the retelling of the tale.

I was tickled. I'm a sucker for first-love-and-first-heartache stories. They seem so much more real than everything that comes before them. Or after them, for that matter. I thanked Simon for sharing his story, and the evening ended on a rather light, rather romantic note.

📖

On Sunday morning, Simon and Jeremy both came out to the driveway to wish us goodbye, as did Leonard and Marti. As the driver threw our bags into the trunk, there were lots of embraces and thank-yous and promises. "I expect a copy of your book," Simon said.

"You've got it," I said.

My last hug was for Jeremy, who said quietly in my ear, "I loved meeting you. You have my number."

"Yes I do," I assured him. And then we were off. Would I see these people again? I couldn't be certain. But then, what is certain? The flight home was mercifully uneventful.

Leonard and Marti showed up at the Walnut Room and other cabaret venues from time to time. It was always fun to see them. Simon did finish the show he told us about, and found a Broadway producer. And Mary *was* great. She got a Tony nomination. We saw Simon and Jeremy backstage on opening night. It was a glorious occasion, of course, as these things always are (even when the show stands to miss the hit mark).

As I hugged Jeremy, he seemed even leaner than I remembered. His eyes were bright, and filled with the excitement of the evening. A Broadway opening is such a rarefied event. But there was also a weariness in Jeremy's face that hadn't been there before. Simon was the man-of-the-evening, so there was no chance of our getting any closer to him than just quick congratulations. As Bobby and I were leaving to make space for other well-wishers, Jeremy mimed a promise of a phone call. Or was he asking *me* to phone *him*? I'll never be certain. And then we headed to Mary's dressing-room.

The show ran for six months or so. I kept meaning to give Jeremy a call. I got so caught up in work and life that I never did. And he didn't call me, either. And then a year passed. And then we heard that Simon was very sick. His death made all the papers, of course. Jeremy's, not so much. And then the memory of them both gradually slipped into that place where all the dead gay boys were filed: that place where the horrors of the decade could be hidden. Out of sight, out of mind? Perhaps. For a while, anyway.

Chapter Four

Peter Prentiss was one of the prettiest people I've ever known. He was medium-height, lean, muscled in a natural sort of way, with dirty-blond hair and vivid green eyes. His lovely, long nose had just the slightest tilt to his left, and the imperfection made him even more appealing. That glorious nose of his saved his face from routine prettiness, and instead projected him into the realm of true beauty.

Peter was a set-designer who had some success Off-Broadway. He had designed a show of Bobby's in the early '80s, and so that was how we knew him. Bobby adored him. I had the hots for him. He had a reputation for being into S&M, which made him even more attractive, as far as I was concerned. We saw Peter fairly often in those years, at various events and benefits. Bobby had another theatre project coming up, and he asked me if I would put together a dinner party. I was delighted to do it. Peter had never been to the apartment, and it seemed high time.

We made date for the next Friday evening, when Peter was free and also his new partner, whom we hadn't met. Since it was still winter, I decided on something hearty: I planned a duck stew with olives and sweet vermouth. Polenta to go with it. Mushrooms and spinach in crisp little phyllo packets to start. And a salad with cheese afterward. I had coffee ice cream in the freezer, just in case. And some amaretti.

Peter arrived, on time, but alone. He was full of apologies, explaining that just before they were leaving their apartment, his partner, Stuart, had gotten a call from a friend who needed him. The friend had gone blind, and Stuart would sometimes go to him, sit with him, and read to him. And that evening the guy had reached out for help, and Stuart couldn't refuse.

"That kind of need makes a dinner party look frivolous," Bobby said. "Anyway, we'll all get together some time soon."

"Yes, let's do that, please." Peter said.

Dinner was delicious, and Peter seemed to be having a good time. He even asked for more duck. So, he was either enjoying it or he was an excellent guest. I chose to believe the former. Over coffee, the subject came up—inevitably—of the torture/death of a young German model at the hands of a fashion mogul and his circle. The story had been in the news for several days.

As I was pouring drinks, Peter said, "I knew that guy! We were in a couple of scenes together in the last few years. Well, you've seen the pictures. What a beauty! He really was breathtaking, but so needy. I can take a lot. Once I'm in it. But this guy? I once saw him start to laugh while he was being flogged. Our masters had bound us together, front to front. While *my* master was gently sharing the kiss of the leather with my back, *his* master began to really punish him. The louder the lash, the louder the laughter. And the louder the laughter, the louder the lash. When it was over, he still had a smile on his face. I couldn't bear to look at his back. I have no idea of the extent of the damage. But when I heard that he had been killed, I thought, *How come it didn't happen sooner?*

"I don't mean to sound callous, but that guy was obviously on a collision course with death. And it really sobered me up. If someone that beautiful— and smart—could be that self-destructive, then where the fuck was I headed? For years I thought I couldn't have an orgasm without some intrusion, some insult, some punishment. But then last year I met a guy who is not the type at all, and he fell in love with me. And you know, it's enough. You'll love Stuart, by the way. I really wanted him to be here tonight, but, well, it couldn't be helped."

"Of course not," Bobby said.

I asked, "Why S & M?"

Peter answered, "I don't really know why I like it. No, I don't *like* it. I *hate* it, actually. More pain is the last thing I need in my life. But I think I—used to, at least—*require* it. I can tell you this: My father used to beat the shit out of me, when he wasn't beating the shit out of my mother, or my brothers and sister. By the time I was ten or twelve, if I didn't have at least a fat lip, I couldn't be sure I was loved. And he *did* love us. That's the sick part. We knew we were loved. And we knew we needed—punishment? I guess that was it.

"The dynamic started to change as I grew up, of course. And then one night, when I was a senior in high school and had just turned eighteen, Dad was sitting at the dinner table, drinking, and heading into a familiar scenario. When he went for my mother, the other kids cowered, as usual, but I didn't. Instead, I went for him, spun him around, and said, 'If you ever touch her again, I'll rip your heart out!.' Dad's a big guy, at least two inches taller than me, with heavy arms and big, ready fists. But when he started to laugh, I decked him. I had never slugged a man before—or since, for that matter—and I was afraid I had broken my hand. But it was just bruised.

"He landed on the kitchen floor, looking more shocked than injured. I almost went to help him up, but instead I went to my room and started planning my escape in earnest. The assaults stopped. Cold. I think Dad believed that I would indeed have ripped his heart right out of his chest if he dared to lay a finger on any of us again. And I would have. It's in a movie somewhere—probably a 1940s movie. Bobby, I'm sure you know it. Some movie star—probably Bette Davis—says something like, 'What gives a threat dignity is the unwavering resolve to carry it out.' Well, that's what I had. And Dad got the message."

"You're pretty much spot-on," Bobby said.

"I don't see my family any more than absolutely necessary. My sister's wedding, that sort of thing. Otherwise, I leave them to their life, just as I reserve the right to live mine. I'm just so glad to be out of it. But am I? Who knows. Stuart and I are building a very satisfying life together. You *have* to meet him! Well, we'll all get together soon."

We did get together, the four of us, the next month. And Peter was right: Stuart was every bit as delightful as he had claimed. Stuart was nearly six-feet tall with a really trim body, longish red hair, and liquid-blue eyes. He exuded gentleness the way some people ooze confidence. It was love at first sight for me. Bobby, too, was smitten.

The fact that Peter and Stuart were both so de-lightful—individually and together—made it all the more painful when we learned the following year that they were both sick. They kept their apart-ment for another year, managing to care for each other with some help from a new nurse service that had been set up by Gay Men's Health Crisis. There were also new programs from New York City and New York State—drug plans, rent assistance, that sort of thing—that GMHC helped to coordinate.

I visited a few times, always taking along some food. Cooking for AIDS victims was tricky, because appetites—and digestion—were damped down by intestinal infections and other malaise. All the guys I knew—except the few who went into brain fever and died within a month—suffered considerable wasting. And, of course, that alone was a serious health risk.

The task was to cook something irresistible but not too spicy and to hide as much butter and cream in it as possible. These boys never regained their weight, of course, but the ones who managed to down some rich food stood a better chance of sur-vival. And survival was the name of the game, for who knew if maybe a cure was just days away? I would produce rice pudding, oatmeal cookies, and rich, creamy meat dishes like *Émincé de Veau*. Mac and cheese worked for some. Most of the guys had lost interest in food so much that it was hard to get them talking about it. But for the few who had any appetite left, I was happy to try to reproduce their childhood favorites.

Peter remembered his mom's meatloaf, so I assembled a traditional one with lots of ketchup and sliced onions on top, veering off course just enough to work in a little butter and olive oil. Peter was grateful, and I actually saw him eating before I left that afternoon. So often I didn't really know how many of my creations made it to stomachs and how many languished in otherwise-empty fridges until it was time to give them the heave-ho.

Stuart told me about a lemon pudding his mother used to make, so I poked around and found a recipe in Fanny Farmer that looked as if it would do the trick. It was all about cookbooks in those days, before the Internet revolutionized all forms of research. I doubled the butter, of course. It turned out very well, and Stuart seemed delighted.

When the boys grew too weak to care for themselves—first Peter and then Stuart—they were hospitalized, at St. Luke's. It was an old hospital on the West Side, a bit run-down, and not one's first choice for having a procedure. But St. Luke's had an AIDS ward at a time when few hospitals—nationwide—would treat victims. The staff was so dedicated that my eyes tear up whenever I think of them.

I should mention that the particulars of the HIV infection and its transmission were fairly well known by the mid-'80s. But of course there was always the possibility that there might be other means of contagion, and—even more likely—there were always possibilities of accidents with blood and other bodily fluids in a hospital setting. Brave men and women went about their daily routines, keeping sick people—who were not going to get better—clean, nourished, medicated, and cheerful.

The AIDS Ward at St. Luke's was one of the most cheerful places in New York. When the order-lies were not doing their own stand-up, there were visits from Broadway actors and dancers who per-formed in lounges for any patients who could make it, on foot or wheeled-in. Often the performers just hung out and visited with the patients, one on one.

And there were volunteers. One was an Episco-pal chaplain who had a natural gift for helping people clear the debris of the past and prepare for the next stage. That next stage takes a whole shit-load of acceptance, and she had language and heart that put many patients at ease as they navigated their endings. We met the chaplain, K D Burgess, on our first visit to Peter and Stuart, who had been moved into a room together. We talked, and laughed, and then went out for coffee while the boys were having their supper. Then we three said our good-byes to the boys, and KD went out with us for drinks, and then dinner. And she has been a trusted friend ever since.

📖

Peter and Stuart died within a week of each oth-er. Neither had the slightest will to continue on alone, and so they didn't. We memorialized them both, together. It felt right to celebrate their indi-vidual lives and their union, which had become inseparable. Peter's sister introduced herself to Bobby and me before the service. She came alone. She was divorced, by then, and Peter's brothers and parents had declined to make the trip from Penn-sylvania. "Peter was the only entirely good person I've ever known," she said. "I wish. . ."

"We all do," Bobby said, as he embraced her. Bobby had a sort of grace when it came to helping people in awkward situations. That he had learned compassion and such deep empathy is still a source of amazement to me. With his Hollywood childhood, how could Bobby have arrived at a place of such emotional maturity?

Stuart's family was rather more in evidence, but we didn't really meet them. There were lots of friends, of course. Several of them went to the podium and said heartfelt things about their shared journeys. We laughed, a lot, as people told stories about remembered mishaps, missteps, and frailties.

K D delivered a lovely eulogy to finish up. It wasn't that standard funeral stuff: "In sure and certain hope of the Resurrection. . ." Oh, my God, here it comes: "earth to earth, dust to dust, ashes to ashes. . ." I can stand *anything* but that. *Please,* don't make me go there again!

No. K D spoke of life, and love, and change. And, Hell's bells, what else do we have? Bobby and I left the church hall feeling as whole as possible, under the circumstances.

Chapter Five

Bobby suggested we invite his friend Geoffrey for dinner that spring. I had spent maybe a half-dozen evenings with Geoff before and had found him prickly and fiercely protective of Bobby. This would prove to be a recurring theme, as I learned how many of Bobby's friends were devoted to him—women, in particular, but even men who had never been his lover. And the men who *had* been his lover were equally devoted. And protective. Which was even more astonishing.

I thought carefully about the dinner menu—and when didn't I?—and remembered that the first shad from local waters had come on the market. And so, I bought some shad roe. I decided to pan-sear it—carefully, with many needle-pricks to the mesentery to avoid explosions. I paired it with snow peas. We started with a light pasta dish with a bit of garlic and anchovy and a handful of halved cherry tomatoes. And after the shad roe we had an arugula salad with blue cheese. And then some fruit.

After dinner and coffee, I said, "Bobby got a bottle of Crown Royal for Christmas. Does that appeal?" Geoff said that it did, indeed. I poured some drinks and we headed into the living room to enjoy the buzz. As we settled into our chairs, Geoff said, "I read a shocking story in *The New York Times* today about a homosexual! Well, I'm not a homosexual, I'm an ephebophile." Now, I went to college, and I read Mary Renault, so I got it. Bobby didn't.

"Cadetophile," I offered as a translation. Geoffrey seemed pleased. If I hadn't gotten the reference, then Geoff would have dismissed me from smart conversation forever after. But Bobby was in a different category. His extraordinary talent—and his extraordinary childhood—exempted him from all intellectual snobbery. As far as Geoff was concerned, Bobby's considerable efforts, through the years, to learn about Western culture beyond Hollywood qualified him for special status. I, on the other hand, had to prove my smarts at every turn.

"So, in that case," I said, "I want to hear about ephebes that you have philed. And don't be stingy!" I didn't really expect Geoff to open up and share something deep, something painful, something intensely private. But what I didn't know—and wouldn't have understood at the time—is that Geoff was just then writing his first novel. And so, he was in a place of memory and vulnerability. I did read the novel, two years later. It was interesting enough, and engaging enough, well-written, of course, but somehow less honest than the story he shared with Bobby and me that silly, drunken evening after we had pigged-out on shad roe and gorgonzola.

"My parents enrolled me in one of the best prep-schools in Ontario," Geoff said. "They wanted me to be a proper gentleman—not an English gentleman, of course, because we were Canadian. But a sort of *Commonwealth* gentleman—someone who could fit in anywhere.

"I liked it. I liked the trappings of privilege and a classical education. I was a decent Latin scholar. But I was indifferent to Greek until we studied the *Iliad*, where Achilles lost his beloved Patroclus in the Trojan Wars. Then Greek started to make sense.

"I had a classmate named Gareth—believe it or not. Canadian families do cling to those Arthurian traditions. Gary was so handsome, and so gloriously, youthfully, and effortlessly wonderful, that I fell head-over-heals. I would have done anything for him.

"Gary was pleasant with me, and, I think, genuinely fond. But when I tried to kiss him in a dark corner of the locker room after a game, he pushed me away. He seemed repulsed by it. And without really understanding, I sensed that he was repulsed by *who I am*. And I was devastated."

"How about another whiskey?" I asked.

"You read my mind," Geoff said.

"I knew that Gary would never expose me to ridicule. He was incapable of that kind of meanness. That was not the issue. It was just that I loved him so deeply that I couldn't imagine life without him. And I felt certain that I had stepped over a line.

"Gary was cool with me after the locker-room incident. Distant even. And before long I had to accept that our friendship was over. When we left school for summer recess, he didn't even say goodbye.

"But then something strange happened. We both were growing up in Toronto, and my first week back home, I went to the big old market downtown to get some things for my mother—peameal bacon, chocolate, and such. I had always found the market a fun place to be, with its soaring iron and glass walls and ceiling.

"I was starting to feel very happy, and the darkness of the last half of the school term began to surrender to the bustle and brightness of the market. As I approached Mother's favorite pork butcher, I was shocked to see Gary standing in the queue, obviously on a similar errand. Except it wasn't Gary. I knew he had a twin brother, but we had never met. This was obviously Gawain.

"They were as alike as two peas in a pod, and yet Gawain was not his brother. I sensed the difference from several yards away. There was an openness about Wain that drew me right up to him, to introduce myself.

" 'Oh, so you're Geoff. We meet at last!' Wain said. 'Gary talked about you all the time in the first term, but then I guess you two ended up in different classes in the spring.'

" 'Pretty much,' I said. So, Gary hadn't given me away, not even to his twin brother.

" 'I just have to get a few things, and then why don't we go and get a pop, or something?' Wain asked.

" 'Sure,' I said. We both finished our shopping lists, and then headed to the little lunch counter in the back. 'Tea sounds good to me. What do you think?' I asked.

" 'Tea it is,' Wain said. And as we spoke the usual getting-to-know-you small talk, sipped our tea, and devoured the rich pork buns I ordered, I began to feel a revival of all the warmth that Gary had stirred up in me. Only this time, it was for a boy who seemed to welcome it, a boy who wasn't just tolerating me, but who seemed to be really interested in me; a boy who wanted my friendship. And I realized that, up close, Gary and Wain really looked nothing alike.

"We walked together toward our different streetcar lines, taking a shortcut through a large park. We were walking arm-in-arm as we approached a secluded area with tall trees. I stopped, turned to Wain, and kissed him. He kissed me back. I was so thrilled, I was afraid I would come in my shorts or pee all over myself, or maybe do something even more embarrassing. But instead, I just kissed him some more and then asked him when we could see each other again.

"Wain and I were inseparable that summer. We went swimming, and boating, and we planned long nature hikes. We also kissed a lot and made love as often as possible—not adult love-making, of course. Adolescents don't really understand the glories of the human body, even when they feel the intensity of a psychic bond. We fumbled, mostly, in his little bed or mine, or in sleeping bags in a tent somewhere in a forest. But our intentions were clear, and mutual. And we clung to each other. And we forged a union that seemed unbreakable.

"Could I have another whiskey?" Geoff asked.

"Of course," I answered, and splashed a refill into his glass.

"Late in August, when Wain and I were out hiking, he stumbled on a rough path and went headlong into a gully. When he landed, he was breathless, but still smiling as I scrambled down the embankment to reach him. Wain seemed to be in good shape as we got him up and dusted him off. And then I realized that he was bleeding, on his right side. There was a fallen tree at the bottom of the ravine, and a sharp branch had punctured him, just below his ribs. I was terrified. Wain seemed unconcerned.

"We tied my t-shirt tightly just above his waist to try to slow the bleeding, and then we hurried back into town and the nearest hospital. The people in Emergency looked grave. But I guess they always do. They cleaned him up and decided that he should be admitted as soon as there was an available bed.

"Once they had settled him in, they let me go up to his room for a few minutes. I said all the usual things, like 'Hang in there, kiddo,' and 'I'll be back in the morning to spring you.' One of the orderlies gave me a shirt, and then I headed home, looking none the worse for wear."

Geoff paused, and then sat quietly for a minute with his drink. I would not have pushed him to finish the story, but then he seemed ready to continue.

"When I arrived back at the hospital in the morning, the staff nurse on Wain's floor said I should wait. And then a pleasant young nurse/volunteer walked up to me and asked me to follow her down the hall. I don't know what those girls are called in the US."

"Candy stripers?" I offered.

"That sounds about right. She led me to Wain's room and asked me to wait in the hall, because his mother and brother were with him. The hospital policy was to limit visitors to two at a time. And so, I waited. I would gladly have eaten my head instead of having to face Wain's family, but that was not an option.

"It seemed like hours, but it was probably less than ten minutes until they left Wain's room. 'Hello, Geoff,' Gary said as he extended his hand. That's what young gentlemen do.

" 'Oh, yes, Geoffrey,' Wain's mother said. I won't call her greeting icy. It felt *glacial* at the time. But then, I've never been a parent, so I can't say how I'd behave if I had a wounded child and the possible assailant in my sights.

"The 'candy striper' led me into Wain's room but made it clear that I only had ten minutes. He looked pale and flushed, at the same time, and not quite one hundred percent present. He smiled at me, of course. He always smiled. No human ever had such a smile.

"I took his hand—the one that was not attached to the arm with the IV—and I sat as quietly as possible for my allotted ten minutes. And before I left, I said, 'Wain, I love you.'

"He looked me square in the eyes and mouthed something very like 'love you' before he disappeared into a haze that was drug- or fever-induced. Probably both.

"Could I have some club soda?" Geoff asked.

"Of course," I said, and snapped into host-mode. "Ice?"

"No, thanks," Geoff said, "if you could just splash some soda into my glass. I'm feeling parched." I obliged, of course. And after a healthy gulp, Geoff continued:

"The hospital staff were pleasant, but not exactly committed to extending kinship rights to 'the friend.' There was nothing more I could do, and so I headed home.

"The phone-call in the morning was from Gary, which was very considerate of him. He told me that Wain's fever had spiked in the night and that his body had gone into septic shock. And he had died.

"This was the '60s, for God's sake, when these things weren't supposed to happen! He was just fucking dead. And I wanted to be fucking dead, too. But, of course, it doesn't work that way. I fell into deep grief, and I also fell into deep guilt, determined that the accident was all my fault, that I should have been looking out for him, that I should never have suggested that hike in the first place, that if I had been better at first-aid, we could have saved him.

"Wain's family was stoic. They didn't blame me for his death, as I feared they would, as I felt they should. Even Gary was warmer to me than I believed I had any right to expect. The funeral was horrible. And then, when all the smoke had cleared, instead of facing a separation at the beginning of the fall term, I was now facing a *permanent* separation. I couldn't accept it. Never have.

"So, you can call it arrested development, if you like—my fondness for young men. Am I hoping to find Wain again? Who the hell knows? But the sweetness of youth was snatched right out of my hands. And I won't apologize for wanting to find it again."

"Nor should you," Bobby said.

Geoff turned to me and said, "And now it's your turn, Kitchen Wench."

"That is not going to happen," I said. "Only a fool would follow a story like that."

"Next time, then," Geoff said. "I'll hold you to it."

CB

Geoff *did* find his ephebe, as it happened, that same year, just before Christmas. He met a guy named Ronald, who was slim and boyish and a talented singer. They had at least four really good years together, I think, until Ronald's health started to fail.

He was obviously sick, and yet Geoff was in deep denial. It was difficult to watch. "He has a skin condition, but he's responding very well to treatment." Or, "His doctor says he's getting stronger every day." Or, "Next time we get together, I'm sure Ronald will come with me."

Toward the end, Geoff did something I found deeply confusing: He invited me over to their apartment. For the first time. Not Bobby. Just me. It was some moment when Geoff knew Bobby was working, and so I would be free to come alone. And I made the trip to the West Side, rang the bell, waited for the buzzer, and walked up to Geoff's little fourth-floor apartment.

Poor Ronald was stretched out on the sofa, not only dangerously lean but also covered with herpes and medication. And yet I approached him, bent down, and kissed him, just as we had always greeted each other. He tried to stop me, but the deed was done.

I sat with him for a few minutes. Cadaverous, I would have thought him, except that cadavers usually look better. Ronald seemed resigned. Geoff seemed his usual jocular but acerbic self. I didn't stay long. Ronald obviously needed his rest, and I certainly needed to retreat from the heartache of the situation. As I was leaving the apartment, Geoff said, "I'll walk you down to the door." He grabbed his keys and came out into the hallway with me, and we started the three flights down to the vestibule.

At the front door I hugged him and said my good-byes without any reference to the situation upstairs. I had no words for it. And then Geoff said, "I felt that you two had a right to know, and I didn't think Bobby could take it. But I knew that you could."

I was stunned, not knowing if Geoff saw me as a trusted friend or as a heartless bastard. I hoped it was the former. And to be perfectly honest, I've never quite figured it out. I was mostly numb as I headed home and started our dinner. I told Bobby about Ronald's condition, of course, but without mentioning that Geoff doubted his ability to handle the realities of it.

Ronald's memorial was not far off. We buried or burned so many boys in those years, that the element of surprise was long past. But the loss was fresh each time. And the memories, once stirred from their slumber, might just as well be from yesterday.

Chapter Six

I've always loved cooking—for others, that is. For myself, alone, not so much. One day that spring, when Bobby was on the road, I called our pianist friend Gabe and invited him to dinner. That way I could be assured of a good meal and some good company. Gabe was a charming guy, tall, with soft brown hair, like the Midwestern farmer of your dreams. He was one of the few pianists whose musicianship Bobby respected, and he also liked my cooking. So, I was happy to ask him over. And Gabe was recently single and dealing with some health issues. I suspected it might be about HIV. I hadn't asked. I wasn't there yet. I still waited, well, most of the time, with Southern politesse, for people to volunteer what they wanted known. But that April I was feeling lonely, and I reasoned that whatever might be going on in *his* life, a pleasant dinner at home would be beneficial for Gabe and me both.

There was still a chill in the air, despite the tentative arrival of spring, and so I decided to prepare a *Carbonnade à la Flamande*. It was a favorite of Bobby's and mine, and I thought it would be a good choice to nourish my farmer/artist friend. That afternoon I puttered around the kitchen as usual, browning the beef and caramelizing the onions, and performing all the extra steps that may or may not be essential. I also fussed too much about setting the table and putting new candles in the candle-sticks. I prepared the *Carbonnade* and some parsleyed noodles to go with it, and, to start, an arugula salad with roasted peppers, goat cheese, and a sprinkling of toasted pine nuts. I had some fresh fruit and ice cream in the fridge in case either of us wanted a sweet after. You never know.

I also phoned Bobby in Los Angeles to tell him that I missed him, that I loved him, and that Gabe was coming for dinner. He said, "I get confused about time zones, so I don't know whether I can call you back while Gabe is there, or if we'll be onstage. Anyway, give him a great big kiss from me, and we'll talk tomorrow." We said our good-byes and hung up.

I was starting to feel horribly alone. Scooter was spending the week with his godparents, and I missed him more than I expected to. But the host gene cut in and reminded me of my duties. I plumped sofa pillows and checked the polish on the glass table tops. Five years earlier, I would have been careful to top up the cigarette boxes and check the fuel in the lighters. But I knew Gabe was a non-smoker, and the whole smoking culture had already begun to fade, anyway. So I put a few of our prettiest ashtrays here and there, and then stashed the rest of it. Then it was time to hit the shower.

Gabe arrived fashionably late (that used to be about 20 minutes, but I don't think people do that anymore) with a bottle of wine in hand, and a flower as well. It was a lovely big white lily, and I chose to believe that *he* chose it for its symbolism, its historic association with purity and virginity. I think I even managed to blush as I accepted it. And then I gave Gabe a hearty hug, took his jacket, and directed him to the living room. I put the lily in a vase for the dining table, and opened the wine that Gabe brought—a California Merlot, actually. I also poured him a vodka on-the-rocks (plus one for me, of course.). That was normal life in those days.

We shared cocktails, chat, and laughter, and then a really nice dinner by candlelight. When we both had eaten our fill—Gabe even took thirds on the *Carbonnade*—we retired to the living room. Gabe had once gone to the piano after dinner and played a brooding Chopin étude. I was used to lovely sounds coming from Bobby's Steinway, but when Gabe played it there was a haunting quality that touched me deeply. Even so, I didn't want him to play for his supper that evening. Instead, I brought in coffee, and poured us each a Scotch. We settled in for a quiet visit. When the coffee had been sipped, and the Scotch tasted, I said, "Gabe, I'm becoming obsessed with sex. Hell, becoming—what am I saying? I've been obsessed with sex my whole life. But I don't think people really talk about their sexual experiences that much. I want to know more—about myself, about my friends, about everybody. Would you be willing to share a story from your past?"

Gabe said, "Sure. I might as well talk about sex since I'm not getting any." I topped up his coffee cup, and he took a moment to frame his thoughts. "I'll start pretty much at the beginning," he said. "My mother decided I should have piano lessons, when I was about ten. She signed me up with Mr. Johnson, a bland little bachelor who lived in a tiny house just two blocks from my school. On Wednesdays, I would walk to his house after class.

He would welcome me into his kitchen, sit me down at the kitchen table, and give me a glass of milk and a cookie or half a sandwich or something. Then he always phoned my mother to tell her I had arrived. The lesson started promptly at 3:30, and Mother would arrive to take me home an hour later. She was always five minutes early. You could set your watch by it. It gave her a chance to hear my progress as I played the final exercises of the lesson.

"Mr. Johnson sat to the right of me on the bench and demonstrated the piano runs that I was to parrot. He smelled of peppermints and starch, and it was very pleasant sitting next to him. I had some aptitude, even though I was not a great student. There was just enough accomplishment to give him something to praise in my work. Well, not praise, exactly. He had two versions of 'Uh, huh!' The one with the falling cadence—*Uh*, huh—meant 'back to the woodshed,' and the one with the rising cadence—Uh, *huh*--meant 'finally, a little clarity.' I was eager to achieve the latter, but happy to accept either judgement.

"As we got to know each other better, Mr. Johnson would sit a little closer to me, and sometimes put his hand on my shoulder. I welcomed the attention. When he rubbed my back playfully, after I had actually learned a tricky passage, it felt really good. And when his hand came to rest on the piano bench, cupping my left butt cheek, I was delighted. Mr. Johnson had beautiful hands, with long, slender fingers. He could play me just as skillfully as the piano. I didn't exactly make beautiful music, but the feelings that pulsed through my body when he touched me felt positively lyrical."

"Would you like another Scotch?" I asked.

"Sure," Gabe replied. I poured, and he continued. "On the fourth or fifth Wednesday, as our lesson began, I did something I had never done before. As he demonstrated the exercise, I rested my right hand on his left leg. It was quite casual to start, but as he finished playing, I had moved steadily up his blue-serge until my hand was resting very close to the little bulge in his trousers that was now becoming a big bulge. He had finished his demonstration, and yet I still sat close to him with my hand on his thigh. I had no intention of removing it. I sat resolutely still, peering down at Mr. Johnson's crotch and waiting. For what, I didn't know, but I was willing to wait as long as it took for some initiation into the mysteries of maleness. When there was no longer any question of where this was headed, Mr. Johnson asked, 'Would you like to see it?'

" 'Yes, please,' I replied.

" 'Very well, then,' Mr. Johnson said, and carefully unbuttoned his fly and took out his Johnson, which was now fully erect. I was mesmerized. Ever the Aristotelian, Mr. Johnson asked, 'What do you think?'

"What I *thought* was that it was the most beautiful thing I had ever seen. What I *said* was, 'May I touch it, please?'

" 'Yes, of course,' he answered. It was, after all, about education.

"I timidly reached out and wrapped my baby fingers around his adult dick. It felt so warm and strong. I got a charge from the contact, just as surely as he did. I cautiously explored his penis—which, looking back, I suspect was just a bit on the small side, but perfectly straight and proud. I moved across the landscape, stopping to finger the ridge around the head, testing the capacity of the peehole with my pinky finger, marveling at the whiteness of the shaft, the blue of the veining, and the extraordinary pinkness of the glans. I added my left hand to the exercise, carefully examining and testing. I cupped his balls, one in each hand. If I had been in playground mode, I would probably have squeezed them, and much too hard. But I was in another dimension—one that inspired care and respect. I explored the various skin textures, all so different, from the scrotum to the shaft to the head. Mr. Johnson was silent. As I continued my exploration, he seemed to be frozen in his focus on me, my hands, and the tiny drama that was playing out right there in his lap. And then he extended his left arm and pulled me ever so slightly to him. I had never felt so close to another human. It didn't matter that I had no idea how to stimulate a dick properly. I just continued to touch Mr. Johnson until he began to breath heavily and to quiver a bit.

" 'Don't be frightened,' he said, as his whole pelvis began to pulse and he expelled wave after wave of hot white jism. I had never seen it before, so I *was* frightened—for a few seconds. But I got over that *really fast*. I was too shy to touch his ejaculate—that time—but my little ten-year-old head was close enough to Mr. Johnson's crotch that I could savor his clean, masculine scent, softened by his lavender body talc, and now overlaid with the irresistibly sweet smell of sex. I knew right then and there that I wanted more. I couldn't have known that Mr. Johnson had just set me on my life's

course, but I knew that something profound had
happened.

"He cleaned himself with his handkerchief, and
then straightened his clothing. 'We've had a very
different lesson from the one I planned for today,'
he said.

" 'Yes, very different," I affirmed.

" 'Is it something you would like to pursue?' he
asked.

" 'Yes, Sir,' I said.

" 'Your piano lessons take priority.'

" 'Yes, Sir.'

" 'We could have more lessons like this one, if
you wish."

" 'Yes, Sir. More lessons like this, please,' I replied.

" 'It would have to be our secret, of course.'

" 'Yes, of course.'

" 'Are you certain you want to start this new
study with me?' he asked.

" 'Yes, Sir!' I replied.

" 'Very well. Then we shall have more of these
new lessons. But for now, Mozart is waiting.'

"We returned to our practice as if nothing had
happened, and we were deep into scales when
Mother arrived, as always, at 4:25. I said nothing—
to anyone—about the incident. I wanted to keep
the secret just as fervently as Mr. Johnson did. It
was mine, or rather, ours. And there was no one
else in my life to share it with.

"The following week, I felt really shy as I arrived
after school for my lesson. But Mr. Johnson was
his usual pleasant but quiet self as he called Mother to tell her of my arrival. I had my milk and
cookies as before. And then we went to the piano.

As we started the lesson, I played something particularly well, and Mr. Johnson hugged me. I
hugged him back. It would have been a quick
thing, except that the only place I wanted to be at
that moment was wrapped in his embrace. I was
not about to let go. He carefully enfolded me in his
arms, and then he kissed me—first on the forehead,
then on the tip of my nose. So, when he got to my
baby lips I was more than ready for his kiss. It was
very tender and gentle, as if he was kissing something precious and fragile, as indeed he was. I felt
just a trace of his beard stubble on my face. I liked
it. I wanted more.

"Mr. Johnson said that, if I agreed, we could de-
vote twenty minutes each week to our new studies,
and not a moment more. I agreed. I would dash
out of school at the first clap of the bell, and run to
Mr. Johnson's house. The time was so precious. I
would gladly pass up a snack in favor of our new
studies. And then we went to the piano promptly at
3:30. Mr. Johnson was adamant about a proper
piano lesson each Wednesday. He was too professional to let anything interfere with my studies."

"Another Scotch?" I asked.

"Well, maybe a splash," Gabe answered. "I live
this story every day, but it's been a long time since I
revisited the whole thing. Let me get back into the
time line.

"Mr. Johnson structured our bedroom studies
as carefully as our piano studies. He would decide
what I was ready for, and when I had achieved sufficient proficiency to move on to the next lesson.
We tried many different things, and Mr. Johnson
never asked me to do anything that I was not more
than eager to try. Then, as now, anything I could

touch went right into my mouth. The first time I experienced the joys of fellatio, my little mouth could just barely accommodate his dick-head. But I was fervent, if not capacious, and I earned my liquid reward. The first time I tasted semen, it was as if I had been served a fabulous new dish. Now, that was a wonderful dinner you made, but I have to admit that *nothing* has ever thrilled my taste buds like a man's essence. I wanted more. I was lucky that my first sample came from a man with very tasty cum—slightly sweet, slightly salt, with a trace of minerality, and not even a hint of the bitterness and off notes that can mar the tasting experience in some men.'

"Mr. Johnson would also go down on my little dick, taking it and my baby balls into his mouth. The warmth of that oral caress was amazing. I had discovered masturbation a few years before, so I knew how an orgasm felt. Even a baby orgasm with no product to show for it is pretty amazing. But when I came while Mr. Johnson's mouth was still warmly containing my young genitals, I was transported to a new place in Pleasure Land. And then there was Prokofiev.

"The first time he bent me over his little bed and pulled down my pants, I was nervous, I admit. But he talked me through it. 'It will hurt, but you mustn't give in to fear. I am here to guide you each step of the way. Take deep, steady breaths, and let your breathing help you focus on relaxing all your muscles. It need not be perfect, and it need not be today. All in good time.' I tried to relax, and yes, it did hurt. But Mr. Johnson was so gentle. That first time we spent most of our twenty minutes with his dick pressed lightly against my baby sphincter.

I wasn't quite ready. But the pressure felt wonderful.

"The next week, too, was tentative. I wanted it so badly, but I still couldn't quite accept something that large. I almost thought I could take him, but it wasn't to be. Still, Mr. Johnson told me he was proud of me. That made me feel as warm as if he had come all over me. Warmer. The next days were agony. All I really wanted was to continue our education. And all I could actually have was school, family meals, and the weekend at Gramma's house. I survived the wait, though I doubted that I could.

"The following Wednesday, after the usual greeting, Mr. Johnson took me up to his bedroom and asked me to take off all my clothes, while he took off all of his. I obeyed his request immediately, with relish. We had never before encountered each other, one-to-one, fully naked. Mr. Johnson's body was nothing like the men in the muscle mags I had seen. He was slim, but not toned, by any means. In fact, he looked a bit soft around the edges. But there was a gentleness about him. And he had very pretty nipples. And he was a man—with pubes and armpit hair, and a perfectly nice three-piece set. And he was real. And he wanted me. And he wanted to be a part of my life. And he wanted what was best for my education. And I think at that moment I realized that I loved him intensely. Whatever that might mean. I didn't think of it as a forever kind of love. I don't know if children can grasp that concept."

"Maybe just another drop of Scotch?" I asked.

"Hell, why not?" Gabe answered. "We're going to have to pour me into a taxi soon anyway. Where was I?"

"Just about to get under Mr. Johnson, I think," I answered.

"Exactly. Mr. Johnson laid me face-down on his bed, and topped me with his whole body. The pressure and the warmth were reassuring. Our time together was very short, and I think we both knew this would be a very special lesson. He moved down the bed and applied his mouth to my little rosebud, giving it a wonderful, warm bath. Then, when he topped me again and gently pressed his penis to me, I was finally ready. He pushed forward with just a bit more certainty than before, and I welcomed him in. The pain was so intense, I gasped. He offered to pull out, but I urged him to go deeper. And he did. And then he was all the way inside me.

"The swirl of intense pain and intense pleasure was like nothing I had ever felt, and nothing I have ever experienced since. Mr. Johnson paused for several minutes, his torso arched so gently against mine, touching at all points but not intruding anywhere except where I craved his intrusion, until I had accepted him fully. And then he began soft and rhythmic movements that strummed every nerve in my body. And before long I felt the now-familiar quiver and crescendo that told me he was coming to a climax. And he did. And for the first time in my life I had a man's dick and his orgasm deep inside my body. Mr. Johnson became very still except for the throbbing in his groin. I felt every pulse. I counted them. The first, strongest ones were the most thrilling. But even as they tapered

into gentle waves, I still welcomed each tiny erup-
tion. When all was stillness, I began to feel sad. I
wanted it to last forever. But, of course, our twenty
minutes were up, and so it was back to the piano.

"I studied with Mr. Johnson for over four years.
So, he was with me through the most awkward
stages of puberty. He seemed to enjoy watching me
grow and change, not always for the better. But
when I was snarky and rebellious, he was patient.
He was always affectionate, but never overly familiar. There was no question that he was the teacher
and I was the pupil, even when I grew to be almost
a head taller than he. That last year, our sexual
explorations began to change as I grew. He made it
a point to spend a few minutes of our precious
twenty assessing my new growth. He said my dick
grew an eighth of an inch each week. He said he
enjoyed measuring my progress, the same as my
progress at the piano.

"It felt great, of course, when he went down on
my raging teen hard-ons. But what I always wanted most was to learn how to better serve my
maestro, to honor him, to pleasure him, to justify
his trust in me. I even started to play better piano.
I would have gladly done anything to be of service.
Mr. Johnson was on the receiving end the first time
I produced a tentative drop of semen. He approached it with respect. He congratulated me. I
felt such pride! It was as if I had mastered a De-
bussy Prelude. And within a few more months I
began to produce a more proper volume of cum. I
shoot a respectable load, I can tell you. I could
show you, actually, but it's so late and you've gotten me drunk, so maybe another time. My point is,
that however I overtook my teacher in height and

girth, I was never able to match the generosity of his emissions.

"It may sound stupid, but he had so much to give, and he gave it—every time he went to the piano, every time he embraced me. No man I've met since has matched it, much less exceeded it. I'm not saying that copious cum is the most important thing in life, even though it feels like home to me. I'm just saying that that sweet little man could have filled a stadium with his offering and still been modest about it. And that quality reinforced my love. As years went by, I always expected my partners to measure up to that high standard. Jim came *so* close. I could have loved him with my whole heart. God knows I tried. No, that's not true. I *did* love him—simply, generously, completely. If only he had been just a bit more—I don't know. Available?

"I never expected a lover to come like a geyser--well, maybe I did years ago. I just want him to be willing to give up his essence, from his gut. Without hesitation or reservation. I've learned that drops of cum, cups of cum, it doesn't matter. It's all in the intention. *It's about the gift!* If he doesn't have the intention deep inside, if he can't *give* from the center of his being, then buckets of cum won't fix it. Well, maybe *buckets!*. But in the end, it doesn't matter how hot he is. It's all about the connection. Does that make any sense?"

"It does to me," I said.

"Once, that year, Mr. Johnson said something that puzzled me at the time, but that's crystal clear in my memory. He said, 'Your testicles have grown to be exceptionally fine.' I was unaccustomed to such praise, and so I felt a bit off-balance. 'You must always cherish and protect them,' he said, 'for they will help to shape the man that you become. And when you find lovers in the future, you will know it is right when your lover is awed by their beauty and determined to honor them.' I developed a new respect for balls that has been with me ever since. A couple of times I nearly fell in love just because the guy had glorious balls. If only they were enough.

"The last month I studied with Mr. Johnson I returned the anal favor that he had first shared so graciously with me a few years before. He seemed surprised that I wanted to do it, surprised that I had grown a near-adult dick of my own, larger than his, even though he had carefully surveyed the growth each week. But he accepted my entry—and even some thrusts that were probably a bit too rambunctious—with the same quiet grace that he accepted all of life: He took it like a man. When I planted my seed inside my beloved teacher, he accepted it with dignity. I, on the other hand, began to weep, like an idiot. But we had spent our twenty minutes, and Rachmaninoff was waiting.

"I would have continued to study with Mr. Johnson, except that there was a whiff of scandal that was not *really* about me, but that *suggested* some impropriety. Small towns are good at that. And so he left. There was no drama. He simply told me after our last lesson that he was moving away, and that he hoped I would continue my studies. I assured him that I would, even though the studies I most cherished were the ones that had occurred upstairs in his little bedroom. We shook hands, almost like equals. And then I left his house, and he was gone, and I never saw him again. It was over for both of us, and that was that.

"I assured my mother that nothing wrong had happened. She accepted my declaration but would have preferred a better story. I had none to tell. I never breathed a word to anyone about our relationship. And, in fact, you're the first to hear it."

"Gee, thanks, Gabe. That's quite a story," I said.

"He was quite a man. I miss him every day. All these years later, whenever I think about sex—and sex thoughts make up much of my day—my experience with kindly, middle-aged Mr. Johnson on his neat little bed with the noisy springs is still my touchstone. His example was more edifying than anything I saw at home, at school, or at church, I can tell you that."

"We didn't have adults like Mr. Johnson where I grew up. If I had found one, I'd have been all over him," I said. And then I had an *In Scotch, Veritas* moment, and I said, "You know, Gabe, I've always been very fond of you. But tonight, I'm ready to call it love."

"I love that you wanted to hear my story," he said. "Next time, I want to hear yours. And now I think it's time I headed home. Dinner was great. Thank you!"

I said good night to Gabe at the door, safe in the knowledge that our night doorman would find him a cab. I hugged him almost fiercely, but he was a big guy and could easily handle any excess of emotion from the likes of me. He kissed me very sweetly, and then he was off into the night.

After putting some food away and neatening up—as little as possible—I blew out candles and turned off lights and headed to the bedroom with a nice buzz in my head. Scotch, love, good food, a heady blend. And then I slipped into a deep, dreamless sleep, and stayed in that state much later than usual.

Late morning, dragging myself from my warm bed to the kettle and the coffee mill, I thought about Gabe's story—as much as my pulsing head would allow thoughts. After a coffee and a little recovery time, I put Gabe's lily on my desk and settled in to write down everything I could remember from the night before. And here it is. I never intended to write a paean to pederasty, but it seemed to me that Gabe's story was all about trust and education. And I suspect that I could have benefited from that level of guidance and attention. But, we'll never know.

Gabe called that afternoon to thank me again for dinner, as we did in those days. I told him I had been writing, and he said, "Sure. Do whatever you like with it. I don't have anything to hide anymore. Life is too short." And as it happened, *his* life was *much* too short.

When Gabe died, the sadness of it fell over me like a shroud. But I had places to go and promises to keep. So I shook off the new mantle and got on with it. But I have never been able to accept that I can't just phone Gabe and ask him to bring his big, talented, delicious self over to the house for dinner. I would give a lot for the privilege of cooking for him again.

Chapter Seven

Hugh Curtis was deadly attractive. In a very skinny way. In fact, he was the skinniest boy I ever met who was also sexy. And he was. He had a set of skin-and-bones I would happily have jumped, under other circumstances. But since he was a young writer who had been recommended to Bobby by an old friend, that collaborative process had nothing to do with me. And I tried to stay out of the way.

We met Hugh first about two years before, when his mentor called and asked Bobby to interview his young protégé. Grey Aldrich was the older man, and he had been working in television for decades, mostly in set-decoration for network soaps. I think he had known Hugh's mother in college, or some such relationship, and Grey had not only taken Hugh on as a project. but had also given him the spare bedroom in his apartment.

A meeting was arranged. Bobby had a positive reaction. And we went to see a small production of Hugh's latest work, staged by a young company in a church basement over near Port Authority. It was refreshing. It was interesting. It was engaging. Great, it wasn't. But Bobby understood what Hugh was trying for, and offered to collaborate, when the time was right—when the ideas had gelled.

Our lives entwined a bit. Hugh's boyfriend Will—who turned out to be a college classmate of mine—was equally charming. Will was bigger and more full-blown-handsome than Hugh. Blonde, and a pleasure to gaze at. Will was a co-producer of a soap. One year he asked me to cater the show's Christmas party. It was a big event, and it taxed my resources. But we got it done, and I was proud that I could actually pull it off. And it was great fun to see so many of Bobby's favorite soap actors all gathered in one big venue. And the next day I could take the leftover cookies and such to a nursing home. So it was a satisfying experience on several levels.

Will also touted to me the virtues of word-processing, which was still in its infancy. Actually, I have a clear sense of the timeline there, reflected in my own experience: My first book was completed, early in 1984, on my old Smith-Corona (electric) portable from college. And that same year, Will said, "You have to try word-processing. The flexibility! It saves me hours a day." And I did try it: I bought one of those clunky desk-top apparati that looked as if they had been fashioned of spare parts for a Quonset hut. There was a learning curve, yes. But after about six months, I never slipped another piece of paper into a typewriter other than an envelope.

Grey, also, asked me to do a project for TV. On-camera, this time—my *cake* on-camera, that is, not *me*. It was for the Thanksgiving parade, and the premise was so convoluted that I won't go into it. Perhaps if I were really proud of the result, I'd crow about my network debut. I knew the cake would be delicious, but the architecture was challenging.

Grey even brought me blueprints. We went over them carefully, of course, how the thing should look. I planned the cake layers and how they would be stacked and shaved into a sphere. I baked cookie armatures to attach to the sphere. I mixed strange colors into my buttercream, trying to achieve the desired space-age look.

I finished the cake—or rather, stopped working on it—and allowed a delivery team to pick it up. The cake appeared as scheduled the next morning. Apparently. They used it *very* early-on in the parade coverage, and by the time Bobby and I woke up and turned on the TV, we had missed it. Network TV and we missed it! Grey said it looked fine. Without having actually seen it with my own eyes, I'll never be certain. This was in the era before HD. So maybe it *did* look fine. Maybe the foil strips that Grey asked me to use to outline the spines were so dazzling to mid-'80s video cameras that the whole cake shimmered to the point where viewers could not actually see its shortcomings. When the host cut into the cake and took a taste, I'm sure it was easy for him to smile and enjoy. I'd love to have a video clip of that. But I don't. And so I'll never know. And it is not a memory that fills me with pride. We can't always choose our memories. But I digress.

Hugh did get his thoughts organized, and he came by the apartment afternoons, that spring, starting when Bobby got back from LA. Hugh was writing the book for a new musical based on a nineteenth-century melodrama with some iconic characters. I thought it sounded like a good idea. Bobby did, too. The first sample scenes and tentative songs seemed very promising, indeed. But we all know that not every show gets finished, and not every finished show gets produced.

There was a particular thread to the story where the "villain," when he mesmerized the "heroine," had to assume her pain so that she would be free to sing, and be glorious. And the more glorious she became, the more damaged *he* became, until choices had to be made all around. Could he survive another one of those headaches? Could she make it on her own? Could she continue to accept her villain/benefactor's largess while her heart belonged to a handsome young man, the one she probably should have been destined for, after all? Choices, indeed. I was delighted by the possibilities.

Sometimes I would be home in the afternoon when they stopped work, and I'd join them for a chat. Hugh was easy to talk with, and, it seemed to me, exceptionally frank. When the topic of musical theater had been shelved for the day, then any relevant topic might take its place. And since we were all three gay men, the topic of sex was never far away.

Hugh volunteered some details of his sex life: He and Will were regulars at a club that specialized in "extreme" sex acts involving bodily fluids and potentially dangerous forms of penetration. I hope you know I'm not a prude. And I've attended at least my fair share of orgies and other romps. But Hugh's stories frightened me a bit.

I had never thought too much about urine, one way or another, until Hugh began to talk about it. And when he described its depths of flavor, I began to wonder if I had been missing something all my years. When I suggested that it would take *at least a few drinks* to get me involved with that, he said, "Oh, no. That's strictly off-limits. Especially beer: It dilutes the purity of a man's wine."

This was new gustatory terrain for me. I never decided to go there, but I found Hugh's stories riveting. Was this risky behavior? Well, urine is famous for being sterile—to its maker, anyway. What about others? I don't know, and I don't really want to do the research to find out. We're not talking golden showers here. That's tame stuff. *Anyone* might pee or get peed-on in the right situation—in a bath tub, preferably. No, this is deep service that Hugh described. Taking another man's essence into one's body is an act of devotion, of worship. It is reverent, serious, and—perhaps, for some—as compelling as more conventional rites. I think I get it. A little.

There were other rites that Hugh described that seemed a bit terrifying, but there was always a theme of trust and community that went with them. And no matter how out-there it seemed, Hugh taught me—without preaching—that the men who performed these acts were bound by a deep sense of love and respect.

"Last month," Hugh said, "we were at the club one night when I decided to get into the sling. It's a nice one—beautiful leather, well worn and lubricated; good lighting: just enough to focus attention on the drama without being distracting. Will helped me in. I lay back and put my legs up on the chains, and then we tested my positioning: I let my head fall back while Will eased his gorgeous dick down my throat. I was in exactly the right place.

"You never know what to expect from a sling scene. Sometimes it takes a while before anyone joins in. Sometimes there are only a few guys who want to participate. *That* night, a crowd began to gather around my little stage. The first one in was a big guy in leather chaps with a huge dick. I accepted him immediately. My ass was his. I gave it up freely and completely. Other guys touched my body, tweaking my nipples, caressing my torso.

"But my mouth belongs to Will. And that's how we like it. Others moved in close and placed my hands on their dicks. I'll take as many as I can. Guys leaned in from both sides with eager mouths. That kind of attention is nice, of course, but the *service* is always what counts for me.

"As Mr. Chaps climaxed, he leaned forward and embraced me quite tenderly in a gesture of thanks. I was touched by the demonstration. He pulled out, very gently, leaving room for the next comer. And the next comer was a hot little guy who seemed to be part donkey and part piston. I accepted him. I welcomed him, even though his needs were quite different from the previous celebrant. If he wanted to pump at a feverish pace, then so be it. I was there to serve.

"And for my next service, I accepted a man who looked like the biker of your dreams, with tattoos and harnesses and chains. He had big, rough hands, that felt like sandpaper when he grabbed my belly. I didn't mind. All part of the service. And his dick felt great.

"I was beginning to wonder about my stamina, but I accepted number four, who was one of the prettiest black men I ever saw. He was not particularly tall or well-endowed, but his face and his ebony skin were so exquisite that I yearned to serve him. I freely gave this beauty the last of my energy.

I would have stayed with him long past my endurance. He *enthralled* me!

"When Black Orpheus finished, I gave Will the sign, and he helped me up and went with me to the bathroom, where I sat and released the excess of the last hour. I also started to cry. When I came out of the stall, Will grabbed me and asked, 'Are you alright, Darling?'

" 'I feel like such a failure,' I said. 'I know I can serve at least a dozen men. Maybe two. And yet I pussied out after four.'

" 'You're quite wrong,' he said. You were the perfect vessel. You were magnificent. And I've never loved you more than I do at this moment.' "

📖

The show that Bobby and Hugh were working on was never completed. There were meetings, here and there, over the next two years. Sometimes really exciting scenes or songs were finished, and then Bobby would be on the road, or Hugh would be distracted by something else going on in *his* life. And then, in time, it fizzled out. Bobby was disappointed that the project failed, but also resigned to the realities of life in the theater. I was just disappointed.

I happened to run into Grey a few years later—at Bloomingdale's, actually—and he told me that Hugh and Will were both sick. I was saddened, of course, but not as shocked by the news as in some other situations. They both died within the next year. We heard about their deaths, but I didn't really grieve for them. Bobby, too, was so involved in his latest project that there was precious little time for processing the loss. And then the memories of both Hugh and Will went into that place where the other unimaginable losses were locked away. I didn't really feel it until now. And I also didn't search for meaning in their lives or their deaths. Until now. I think some people simply refuse to edit themselves, no matter what. And that is a courageous way to live. Even when it is also foolhardy. I try—really hard—not to judge.

Chapter Eight

Derrick Wilkins was a New York actor Bobby had known for years. He starred on a soap for a decade, and did some important Off-Broadway shows and even the occasional Broadway show that didn't quite make it into the realm of immortality. Derrick was tall, slim, and wonderfully handsome, with dark hair and eyes, and a terrific, rich speaking voice. And a credible singing voice as well. He had also been known to dance when it was required, and there were those who wondered how he could kick up his heels without damaging the famous equipment that he was said to be packing between his legs.

In the interest of full disclosure, I must say I never saw Derrick dance. So, I can't swear to his Terpsichorean skills. But Bobby and I did bed him once, back when we all used to fall into bed together without too much thought. And I can attest that Derrick's equipment exceeded its reputation in size and grandeur. He was also rumored to have affairs with women. Well, I didn't care where that dick had been, I just wanted it!

Bedding Derrick was one of the most deliciously thoughtless experiences of my youth. It was pure fun, and over-the-top in the erotic department. Derrick was entirely present in the moment, whether he was allowing us to worship Priapus, or mounting me with masterful ease and reassurance while at the same time engaging Bobby totally in the scene. I had truly never thought to experience a dick of that size, and yet I took it almost as casually as if it had been any ordinary other. And then Derrick filled me utterly. He drew Bobby into his arms. He embraced us simultaneously as if we three were the only beings on Earth that mattered, at that moment. And, of course, we were.

Afterward, we three plunked our naked selves down on the leather sofa in the living room, and celebrated life and love. We drank, and giggled, and kissed, and almost got ourselves into a re-match. But it was much too late, and so we found Derrick's clothes—in various rooms—and helped him dress while all three of us would have much preferred to keep him *un*dressed. And then he went home. And there was never a repeat performance. Indeed, what would be the point of trying to replay perfection?

But that's all history. *This* year, 1986, Derrick was a friend we saw at events and met for dinner now and then. He was one of my favorite guests, because he was not only hot stuff but also delightful company. He was my go-to guest when we needed an extra man. Just as an attractive woman at a party makes straight men courtly and more attentive to their wives, so an attractive man makes the ladies glow. And when that man was Derrick, they positively beamed.

In late May, when there had been hints of summer but also some mercifully cool days to savor, Bobby and I invited Derrick and my chef friend Clyde for a Sunday supper. I was always a bit nervous about cooking for Clyde, so I decided on one tried-and-true—*Minestrone* Milano-style with rice, served tepid—and then something I had never made before, a chicken braise flavored with the hottest "new" condiment in New York, balsamic vinegar. Fruit and cheese with good bread from Dean & DeLuca would round things out.

Clyde called on Saturday to cancel because a sick friend needed him. Sick friends and care-givers were becoming the new normal, so I was totally understanding. And having Derrick to ourselves was hardly a strain. Sunday evening arrived—and so did Derrick—and the three of us had a lovely, low-key dinner. The chicken turned out well, but I made a note-to-self about how to improve it the next time—more garlic and a splash of red wine vinegar to increase the acidity, mostly. After dinner, we took our coffee into the living room and settled in for a visit. I poured a Jack Daniels for Derrick, a vodka for Bobby, and a Scotch for me. Scooter wandered around a bit, and then settled himself under Derrick's chair and began to snore softly.

I broke the contented silence with my new favorite plea: "Derrick, I've been asking friends for stories about sex—my favorite topic. I don't know, maybe I'll turn them into a short story collection someday. Would you share one?" I asked.

"Sure," Derrick answered. "My favorite topic, too." We finished our coffee and sipped our drinks, and then Derrick began: "About five years ago, I met a guy at a neighborhood bar where I used to hang out. He was young and slim, and had pleasant, sort of average looks. And an easy smile. His name was Bill, and I invited him to my apartment. He accepted, and off we went.

"The sex was good. Not great, but good enough that we agreed to exchange phone numbers. When Bill stood up to slip on his jeans, I was still reclining, with my head propped up on one hand so I could watch him. And at that moment, I realized he had a beautiful ass. Not just a *beautiful* ass. It was maybe the *most* beautiful ass I've ever seen. It was perfectly made, like living marble—warm, inviting, just the right size, just the right proportion. When he moved to put his feet, one at a time, into his pants legs, his butt muscles rippled beneath the marble surface, playing with the depth of those indentations on either side that make butts so fascinating to watch. I kept hoping for a flash of pink, but it wasn't so much the rosy orifice I craved—sweet as it would surely be—but rather the stunning cheeks that guarded it. They seemed so sculptural, and yet, quivering with life.

"Bill finished dressing and headed for the door. I kissed him goodnight with a bit more ardor than perhaps the occasion had warranted. He seemed slightly surprised, but pleasantly so. And then he was off. I think it was at that moment, as I watched him walk down the corridor to the elevator, that I realized Bill's ass was so beautiful that a man could get lost down there and not want to find his way home."

Derrick seemed to glaze-over a bit. I offered another splash of Jack Daniels. He accepted it. "Ah, beauty," Bobby said. And then Derrick continued.

"I called Bill the next day and asked him over on Friday night. He was maybe a little surprised by my call, but happy to accept the invitation. I felt a little flutter in my heart, and a lightness in my body that had been absent for some months. And I also began to fantasize about Bill's ass and all the things I wanted to do to, with, and for it. It was a giddy week. I had a few auditions, but nothing major. Mostly, I was just waiting for Friday. Waiting and day-dreaming.

"I imagined Bill showering, and dressing for work in a little junior clerk outfit: white shirt and narrow dark tie, the gabardine slacks pinching his butt a bit, but still making it look adorable. I imagined him seated at his desk, and I fantasized about being beneath his desk chair. Never mind where that was going. And then my mind's eye followed him to the gym, where he stripped down to bare skin before stepping into a skimpy jock. The narrow elastic straps caressed his cheeks, and I was jealous. But even in my fantasy, Bill went ahead with slipping on some silky gym shorts and a tank top, then his sneakers, and he was ready for the weight room. I forced myself to leave him to his workout.

"The next day I imagined founding a new cult, the Brotherhood of the Sacred Buttocks. I figured since my friend Javier made such great Jewelry he could design a golden mask for us to wear during services. But something was missing. And that's when I realized that nipple rings would unite us. All the brothers would have their left nipples pierced and fitted with a distinctive gold ring— designed by Javier, of course. The more devout would be permitted to have both nipples pierced. But only I could wear a ring in my penis. Perhaps in the future there might be ways for the faithful to earn the right to wear the Holy Prince Albert. But for now, that right would be mine alone.

"I imagined the needle going through my left nipple. The pain was intense, but I wanted more. Then the right. Then the head of my dick. And then I was fitted with the gold rings—Javier's rings—and I felt cleansed by suffering, and ready to serve my God more purely. I considered other installations: the Holy Frenum Ring, the Holy Scrotum Ring, the Holy Guiche. I wanted them all, but I cautioned myself to take it slow. I made all the rules, and I liked it that way.

"I was certain that Harvey Klein, the best costume designer on Broadway—who owed me a favor—would be happy to create ceremonial robes for the cult. Heavy, somber, frontless robes for the celebrants, and a backless robe for the Deity. Bare feet seemed best. I planned the lighting, and the music (very low-key chants). I lusted for our first conclave. I planned the service:

"When the Brothers had gathered, I would lead the Deity to the altar, which he would approach, spreading his feet wide and leaning in toward the table, offering us a perfect view of his divinity. I, as High Priest, would begin the ceremony with the ritual cleansing, performed with my tongue. And then the Brothers could come forward, one at a time, and kneel before the altar to offer their prayers and supplications. The two beefiest Brothers would assist at the altar as Deacons, flanking the supplicants, to maintain protocol and record the particulars of the worship. Brothers who were moved to orgasm would carefully place their offering into a golden bowl—Javier again. The Deacons would duly note the fervor of the worship and the size of the offering. These factors would determine the ranking of the Brother at the next service.

Those with offerings would be permitted a chaste kiss before backing away.

"I would approach the altar as the last of the celebrants. The chants would increase ever so slightly in pitch and volume. My worship would be the most fervent, and my offering the most generous. I would allow the gold ring on the end of my dick to bounce on the rim of the golden bowl as my worship intensified. Only I could provide that heavenly tintinnabulation that signaled the climax. And then the service would end, and the Brothers would file somberly to the vestry to change into their street clothes.

"When I was at last alone with the Deity, he would offer me the Golden Bowl, saying, "For your service, Brother Derrick." I would reverently hold the bowl with both hands, wait for the Deity to pass a blessing over it, and then carefully drink the contents without missing a single drop of the sacramental fluid. Thus nourished, I would be ready to continue my duties.

"It would have been glorious, my cult. I could have lost myself completely in it. With enough converts—and what man could refuse?—I could be assured of purpose and daily sustenance. I figured it made more sense than any other religion."

"May I join?" I asked.

"Of course," Derrick answered. "All men of good will are welcome. But, of course, some are gooder than others. For instance, if you would be willing to officiate in a special role that doesn't have a robe, then I could offer you the position of Cup-Bearer."

I slipped out of my chair and knelt on the carpet at Derrick's feet. "As Your Worship wishes," I said. *You* try saying that after a few drinks.

"Bless you, Little Brother," Derrick answered while placing his left palm on my head. "Your naked beauty will be an inspiration to us all." I settled myself next to his chair with my head on his left knee.

Bobby said, "I want to be the composer. I think you need new music."

"Each according to his gifts, Brother Robert," Derrick said. "And in your case, I'm *also* expecting a generous offering at the altar while our newly installed Little Brother is holding the golden cup."

Well, in the old days we all would have been sucking and fucking in an instant. But times had changed, and there was really no way to go back. Still, I couldn't bear to leave my position there on the floor with my head on Derrick's knee. Even though I knew it wasn't going anywhere carnal, I still needed the closeness. Bobby and I never really talked about it, but I think he understood. We waited quietly for Derrick to resume his story.

"Finally, Friday arrived, as it always does, and Bill showed up—on time, too. I asked him in, took his jacket, offered him a beer, and then got right down to business. The kisses were good. Very good. Better than I remembered. And then we quickly shed all restraints and got down to it on my big old bed. This time I didn't just let nature take its course. No, this time I made a bee-line for Bill's ass. The first time I went down there, I thought I had discovered a new world. I buried my face between his cheeks, and explored boldly with my tongue. Everyone likes being rimmed, I guess. Bill was certainly responsive. I lost track of time, so I have no idea how long I was there. A half hour, maybe? Bill didn't seem to mind, so I just stayed there, contentedly lost in the landscape.

"Eventually, even *I* knew it was time for a change. So, I reluctantly left my newly claimed territory and gave Bill a kiss. He kissed me back. That would have been a delightful pastime to engage in for a while, but instead I put Bill on his stomach and mounted him. I'm pretty big—oh, you two know that!—so I'm always careful to give a guy all the time he needs to accept it. Bill took a few deep breaths and then took me in. We both gasped—he because of the intrusion, and I because I felt that I was home for the first time. It was a glorious feeling. It was maybe the most intense moment of my life. Better than getting a Tony nomination. When I erupted deep inside Bill's flawless butt, he came, too. That sort of thing doesn't happen that often, so I took it as a sign that something important was going on. I think Bill did, too.

"Our next date, a few days later, was not all that different from the one before, except that we had dinner first in the little café around the corner. Getting-to-know-you is always fun. When we got upstairs to my bed, I could tell that Bill would have preferred a little more attention to his front half. He reached out to caress me and explore my body and try to discover what pleasured me, as we all do in a new relationship. You notice I said *relationship*, not quick fuck. I got it. I liked it. But I've always been happier *doing* things, rather than *being done*, and I knew exactly what region I wanted to explore. I wasn't about to give it up. Bill accepted me, and the sex was so good that we both lost ourselves in it, I think, and thoroughly enjoyed the ride."

I stirred a bit. "Would you like another Jack Daniel's?" I asked.

"Oh, no thanks. I promised you a story and I don't want to forget anything.

"For our next meeting, on the weekend, Bill invited me to his place. He managed a little supper from his tiny kitchen, and I was impressed that he went to the trouble. His apartment was small and cramped, but the bed was big enough for two, and it had Bill in it—Bill and his beautiful butt. 'I do have other body parts, you know,' Bill said as I went for my new favorite position. He did, indeed, and I was happy to explore them. He smelled great, for one thing. We all know the cliché about velvety skin, but Bill had it. His chest was so smooth, almost like an adolescent boy's. His limbs were lean and nearly hairless but for a light dusting of golden down. I could have spent hours on one of his armpits alone. The little thatch of golden-brown hair tickled my nose, and the taste—ever so slightly salty—was delicious. Bill's manly parts also had a boyish look—a well-hung boyish look, that is. In short, he was totally endearing, right up to the way the hair curled on the nape of his neck. All this I saw, and tasted, and savored. But I kept being drawn down to adore that ass.

"Before I left Bill's apartment I suggested that we meet later in the week at my place for take-out and, whatever. He hesitated, for the first time. But then he accepted, and I headed home with just the slightest feeling of uneasiness. Was I on probation? Was Bill considering if I deserved another chance? At what? I had a vague notion of wanting to adore his entire being, but his soul, his essence, and the rest of his perfectly nice body all seemed to disappear when I was down between those thighs.

"That Thursday evening, after our takeout from Balducci's, I tried, I really tried to be a generalist. God knows I wanted to continue my adoration, and I was willing to do anything to keep that option open. I spent several minutes just on Bill's lovely balls. I could only just barely fit them both in my mouth at the same time. I caressed them as gently as I could, and loved every moment of it. I took his dick in my mouth. It was firm and strong, with just the very slightest downward curve, so it slipped effortlessly down my throat. I took it all. I *wanted* it all. I was content to share that union, only coming up for air when absolutely necessary.

"How long was I there? How long should a lover engulf his lover's cock? Please, don't ask *me*. From there, I ran my tongue over Bill's flat belly and explored his navel. It was very cute. I continued on the path up his lean chest, stopping to savor each nipple. They were rather small, but standing at attention. I nibbled and nuzzled, and it was good. Then I kissed Bill deeply. It was *very* good. I could imagine doing it again, often, for a life-time, even.

"And then I went down to the sacred place, and I was lost. If there had been a fire alarm, I wouldn't have heard it. Nothing mattered but that act of devotion. I think that was it. I think Bill knew for certain at that moment that it was not *really* about him. As much as I *wanted* it to be about him, it was about his *ass*! Afterward, Bill left my apartment quietly, and I had no idea what to expect from the future.

"Bill called me the next day and suggested we meet for a drink. I accepted. We got a little table in the corner, where it was quiet enough for talk. Bill said, 'Derrick, I really like you, but I can't see you anymore.' I was shocked and speechless.

" 'Buttocks do not a relationship make,' Bill said.

" 'In your case, I think we could disprove that,' I said.

" 'I want more, Derrick. I'd even settle for a man who just wanted my whole body. No, that's not true. I want the whole package.'

" 'I would gladly worship your whole package,' I dared to joke.

"Bill smiled his easy smile, in spite of himself, and it gave me hope that I might still have a chance. But then Bill said, 'Thank you, Derrick, for the fun times we've had, and for wanting more. So did I. But I just can't do this. I'll miss our dinners and our dates. I'll miss *you*. Good night. Good bye.' And then he was most certainly out of the bar and out of my life."

"Did you ever. . ." Bobby started to ask.

"No, never saw him again. Well, let's not be *too* dramatic. Of course, I ran into him a few times in the following years. We were practically neighbors. We always smiled and said a mouthed hello from across the street or across a room. But we never really spoke again. I guess I'm just another man who loved not wisely but too well."

"And thank you, Professor, for our drama lesson for the evening," Bobby said.

"Yes, thanks, Doc," I said.

"Glad to be of edification," he answered.

I was still sitting on the floor at Derrick's knee. I would gladly have slipped between his legs and gone right to that extraordinary dick that he was

84

hiding, not very successfully, in his trousers. I wanted it. I was ready for worship. I was ready for anything. Bobby came to my rescue. "Sunshine, why don't you wrap up the rest of the *Morbier* for Derrick to take home with him. We'll never eat all that cheese." I was saved. I returned to reality and became a host again.

Derrick said his goodbyes and Scooter reanimated himself—as dogs always do when things are ending. Poor Scooter got the short version that night—just a visit to the garden. I vowed to give him an extra-long walk the next afternoon.

We only had one more delightful dinner with Derrick, at a hot new Italian restaurant in the Flatiron neighborhood. I didn't like the food very much, so I won't tell you the name—it still packs them in nightly. Even so, it was a treat being with him, as always. I guess he made me beam just as surely as he stirred the ladies. I always smiled more after an evening with Derrick. When I dream about him— and I do—he is part Pied Piper, part d'Artagnan, and part St. Francis. Don't ask me why. I can't explain it even to myself.

We were horrified—but no longer surprised— when we learned a few months later that Derrick was sick. There was nothing that anyone could do, least of all Yours Truly. That feeling of helplessness—on the part of victims and survivors alike— had the power of a recurring nightmare.

Derrick went fast. Some did. Within six months he went from the appearance of robust health and good looks to a wasted, cadaverous frame with a fevered brain. Death was the only possible mercy. It did not elude him long.

As usual, I left the loss largely unprocessed in my heart. As much as I ducked the reality of his death, I also had a keen sense that Derrick was the owner of a bright flame that once extinguished could never be replaced. I feared that New York would become a darker town. And it did.

Chapter Nine

Spring was mostly cool that year. Very few of those false summer days that always sap my energy. When an old friend of Bobby's called to say he would be in town for a few days, I was pleased to ask him over. And whatever turn the June weather might take, the air conditioning was behaving nicely. It didn't always, but that year it was solid.

Robbie Prescott had lived in Manhattan for most of the '70s. Bobby knew him because he worked for a talent agency, which then sent him to Chicago. He was mostly a literary agent, but he also had clients who were artists and performers. I met him just before he left town, and found him engaging in a slightly distant way. And very attractive, in a decidedly WASPy way. I like WASPy men, when they're sexy. And Robbie certainly had the S gene.

I was drawing a blank on menu ideas until I remembered some Cantonese dishes that a colleague had recently taught me to make. A whole steamed fish—what fun! Roast pork for an appetizer, and then the fish with a substantial vegetable dish to go with it, maybe with a few shrimp thrown in, something I could wok while the fish was steaming. Rice of course. And then fresh fruit for dessert.

Robbie arrived, and it was a pleasure to see him again. He and Scooter had never met, and that introduction went well. I found Robbie more handsome than I remembered, but a touch sad. He and Bobby shared an old-friends embrace that was lovely to see. And we settled in for drinks and catching-up gab.

Dinner went smoothly. The steamed seabass was one of my proudest offerings. The flesh lifted right off the bone, leaving a spine that glistened with life. Well, not life, exactly, considering. But it was moist and translucent, and there were traces of miniscule blood vessels here and there. So I knew that it was perfectly done. And it was also delicious. And my wok job was fine. The air-conditioning held. The evening was looking successful.

I'll drink tea, happily, when I'm in an Asian restaurant, but at home I always prefer coffee after dinner. Bobby, too. And guests seem to prefer it as well. I brewed an imported Italian coffee that I had never tried before, and it was actually quite nice. And, of course, you know, we also had a well-stocked bar. Robbie took a Drambuie. And I joined him. Bobby was a vodka man, of course. Scooter surveyed his options, and then chose the middle of the living-room rug for a serious nap.

As we were finishing our coffee, I said to Robbie, "I don't really know very much about you. Bobby loves you, so you have to be special. That's a given. But could you fill me in, a little, maybe?"

"He wants a story, Robbie. Sorry about that. He's collecting them. I can't see that you have much choice, after that dinner. What do you think?"

"I think that I would be delighted to comply. There's actually a story that I've been reliving on a daily basis this year. And maybe if I share it, out loud, then I'll be able to set it aside a bit. Anyway, Drambuie is lovely, but I think I'm ready to move on to the real thing. I might need it."

I poured Robbie a Scotch (and one for me), and he began:

"The summer after we graduated from college, my friend Helen, who was easily the most beautiful woman I've ever known, decided that she wanted a baby. But not a husband. This had been done, of course, so we were certainly not shocked. She looked over her men-friends, and went Eeny, Meeny, Miny—and Moe turned out to be my friend Jonathan. Jonathan is such a delightful man, and smart, and so effortlessly pretty. And he has a huge dick. *I* would have been more than happy to bear his child, so I felt that Helen had made the right choice.

"I was the alternate, as it happened, just in case Jonathan's swimmers couldn't cross the finish line. I figured I'd always have that on my record. Not first, but second place. Respectable. Solid. And the other two men—one I knew fairly well and one I had never met—knew that they were the backup team. Just in case. Helen knew exactly what she wanted—as always—and this was not going to be a turkey-baster event. No, this was going to be a *conception*, and it was going to be perfect.

"On the most auspicious day—based on calendars, and thermometers, and probably other signs—we were all summoned to Helen's apartment. A two-bedroom apartment, fortunately. Helen retired to her room with two girlfriends, and we four boys went to the other bedroom. We undressed and began to prepare Jonathan for the rite. We rubbed him down with a dilute solution of rose water and glycerin, and then we braided flowers into his hair. Tiny little lilies, I think. He had such wonderful, long hair in those days. It was all the rest of us could do to keep from jumping him on the spot. But we all knew there were other plans for Jonathan's energies that day, and so we tried to focus. There was still a little time for the three groomsmen to prepare, as well. So, we created a team of *four* naked celebrants who were scented, and beflowered, and ready to serve.

"When the knock came on the bedroom door, we led Jonathan to the altar. I took his left hand, our friend Douglas took his right, and the fourth guy, who I had just learned was named Christopher, brought up the rear. We proceeded to Helen's bed with reverence and measured (bare-foot) step. Helen was lying in a stately pose, on lots of pillows, with her two attendants flanking her. She was also festooned, of course, and the bed was strewn with rose petals. Doug and I led our best friend to the sacramental bed, and placed him on top of the goddess, helping him into position, helping his stunning dick into the sacred target.

"We three groomsmen remained throughout the rite, caressing the blissful couple—especially the *male* half of the blissful couple—until Jonathan had delivered on his promise. When the tension subsided, we three extras pulled back, a bit, awaiting further instruction. One of Helen's girlfriends said softly, 'And now, the others.'

"It had never really occurred to me that the rest of us might be called upon to perform *today*. *The Alternate* would be next, of course! And It wasn't just that I feared the flowers in my hair had wilted. Helen considered her options, I'm sure. Three more potentially viable strains of DNA might improve her chances of conceiving. But she said, to my great relief, 'No. This is perfect. And we can always re-convene next month, if necessary.'

"Doug and Christopher and I led Jonathan from the breeding bed, and then we withdrew to our dressing room, while Helen remained quietly with her attendants. Lie back, knees up, wait for the strongest swimmers to pass through the cervix, op-timize the opportunities, that sort of procedure.

"But we boys fell into bed together, and giggled, and carried on as boys do when they are suddenly released from the need to be somber. I even went down on Jonathan and got my first taste of a man who has just been inside a woman. I liked it rea-sonably well. I resolved to try it again. There wasn't really much that I *didn't* want to try, in those days, and when Christopher came over to me and kissed me deeply and then lay down beside me, I wanted to try a *whole* lot more of *that*.

"Chris and I made-out for a very pleasant span, until everyone realized that it was time to leave. And even Chris and I had to accept that we should dress and go. We paused at the throne, Helen's throne, on our way out, of course. We offered kiss-es, and bowed, and promised our complete loyalty to the cause. And then we left.

"Chris came home with me, and then we made love in earnest. And then we decided to give that a try for, like, maybe a lifetime.

"The rite was successful, by the way, and the offspring of that ceremony that we all shared with such joy just graduated from Harvard last June. I attended the service. Helen was there, of course. Jonathan would have been there, except that he had to be in Hong Kong on business. The girl-friends had mostly drifted away, I think. Douglas is living in San Francisco and just couldn't get East that month. It was very grand, as graduations always are, especially Ivy League graduations.

"I would have felt so much more pride in the celebration if Chris had been by my side as our godchild, Elizabeth, marched up to the podium to accept her diploma. But I had approved the arrangements for Chris's cremation the month before. I only attended the graduation just to see if I could do it, and to see if there was anything left of my heart.

"When Elizabeth hugged me after the ceremony and said, 'Thank you for being here, Uncle Robbie,' I figured that I might actually still be alive, after all. I felt the pressure of her embrace, and I felt the sweetness of marking life events with ceremonies. And what was left of my heart went out to her, for our shared history, for her youth, for new beginnings. All of that.

"Helen and I went to lunch afterward in a nice little café in Cambridge. She looked great. She smelled great. And I realized that she was even more beautiful than when she was in her twenties. She was just so *together*, as always, and it made me wonder if I was just getting *older* while she was getting *better*. We had a glass of wine, and after the waiter had delivered our salads, she said, 'You were my first choice, Robbie.'

" 'What?' I asked.

" 'I wanted you to father my child.'

" 'Why are you saying this?' I asked.

" 'Because it's the truth, and because I thought you had a right to know.'

" 'And?' was about all I could manage.

" 'I wanted a child desperately, as you know. And I wanted her—as it happened—to be *mine*. Only mine. And I knew that if she were *ours*, then you would have wanted to be her father. You would have wanted to marry me. You would have wanted to do all the right things. You would have wanted to reshape *your* life and *mine* into *your* idea of how these things should be done. You would have been *involved*.

" 'I'm not saying there's anything wrong with that. Look at the home you made for Chris. He *thrived* because of it. You know what a horrible childhood he had. Chris was so—damaged. And wonderfully affectionate, despite it all. And at times, I thought that perhaps he was the most beautiful man I knew. Jonathan was, well, *obvious*, in comparison. Chris was *deeply* beautiful. I never told him that. I hope someone did. I hope *you* did. And when you told me that you two were together, I rejoiced. You saved him. He would never have been so, so, *complete* without you. And he would never have lasted as long as he did. It's who you are.'

"We toyed with our food for a bit, and then asked the waiter to take it away. We ordered some coffees and a sorbet. 'But, Jonathan,' I said, 'You wanted him.'

"Helen lit a cigarette, took a deep drag, and said, 'Oh, Robbie, you know better than that. Jonathan is handsome, and precious, and because we love him, we accept that he is who he is, and that he's only as available as the last time we've had him in our arms. I knew that he would be charming and distant. And that was what I wanted. I prayed that he would give me Elizabeth. And he did.'

" 'I could have given so much more,' I said.

" 'And so you have, God damn it!' she said. That's what I'm trying to tell you!'

"We sipped our coffee and took a breather.

" 'Listen to me,' Helen said, 'I adore you. Always have. You didn't know that? You're the best man I've ever known. Elizabeth adores you. Always has. You didn't know that? And Chris *worshiped* you! I wanted to be a little old lady with an invitation to your 70th anniversary party—80th would have been even better. Well, *fuck it,* it didn't work out that way. So, what's next? Where is that heart of yours going? Chris wrote to me last year.'

" 'Please, Helen, don't do this.'

" 'He said, "Robbie will be so sad when I die. Please don't let him be alone. Please make him get back into it. Find some cute young guy for him to love." '

" 'I don't believe you,' I said.

" 'I swear on Elizabeth's diploma,' Helen said. 'And her birth certificate.'

"I began to weep softly. Helen put her hand on mine and said, 'I know, Sweetie.' She waited patiently for me to get myself together.

" 'I don't know how to do it,' I said.

" '*Of course*, you don't,' Helen said. 'But you will. And when you do, you'll get back into life, and you'll be fine. Robbie, I'm afraid I must run. I've been summoned by Elizabeth's grandmother. You're lucky you missed her at the service this morning. But it seems I can never escape the Iron Lady. Thank God, I'm nothing like her. Am I? No, don't answer that! I'll tell her you send regards.'

" 'Yes, please do,' I said. 'Helen, I love you.'

" 'It was always you, Robbie. Always *you*. Don't forget that. Gotta run!'. And she was off.

"Well, God bless her. Helen can certainly make things happen. Breeding, I think. I still haven't found a cute young guy to love, though I'm open to the concept. But Helen was right: I did figure out how to live again, eventually. I simply decided that Chris is with me always, just as he was in life. And that's how I do it."

I thanked Robbie for sharing his story. And I asked him if I could write it down. He said, "It's all yours."

"No, it's all *yours*," I said. "But thank you for trusting me with it." And then I couldn't resist adding, "I don't have much experience as a matchmaker, but I'd take you on in a heartbeat. I want you to find that loveable guy, too, Robbie."

"I'm just about ready," he said.

📖

And so he was. In the fall, when he visited again, Robbie brought a delightful man named Charlie to the apartment with him. And Bobby and I were both thrilled for the two of them. Relationships are not easy. Nor is loss. Connection eludes some people. But when we're ready, wonderful things can happen.

Chapter Ten

"We haven't seen Kevin in ages," Bobby said that July. "Why don't you invite him to dinner?" Bobby was right, and I got on the phone to Kevin and invited him for Saturday night. I decided to make a cold avocado soup—rich-tasting but with no cream—and *Vitello Tonnato*, a great favorite of ours. I thought about making some fruit sorbet. I had once made one with kiwis that was terrific. But in the end, I decided to *buy* some sorbets. And we were all set.

Kevin Fuller was a talented clothing designer. Shoes, belts, and handbags, mostly. The line was low-key, but available in some of the most expensive stores. He was also a theater-lover, and so that's how we met him, when he came backstage after a performance of a show that Bobby was trying out Off-Broadway. Kevin was medium height, with an unruly shock of auburn hair and a glorious big smile that revealed a collection of exceptionally pretty teeth. It was love at first sight.

I always thought Kevin was one of the sexiest men I knew. Bobby concurred. We never bedded him, for some reason, even though we met toward the end of the wild '70s. It just didn't happen, and then we were now well into an era where that brand of casual sex no longer seemed appropriate—or safe. I was totally capable of enjoying my friends without fucking them, and Kevin was delicious to be with, even without tasting.

He arrived for dinner, armed with some *Montélimar* nougat from a new shop downtown. His presence always brightened the atmosphere, and I felt a happy buzz all out of proportion to the amount of vodka I had consumed. Dinner was pretty, and cool, and really delicious. I was proud of my creations, and Kevin even had seconds. We took our coffee into the living room after dinner, and I poured drinks—our usuals and some gold rum for Kevin.

"Could I ask a favor?" I said.

"You'd better accept him, Kevin. He's relentless," Bobby said.

"Now I'm intrigued," Kevin said.

I said, "It's just that I'm asking friends for stories about sex. Maybe I'll get around to writing a collection. Not certain yet. But would you share?"

"Of course. Do you want the truth, or fantasy?" Kevin asked.

"Your call," I answered.

"Then I think I'll go with the truth." We finished our coffee and started in on our drinks. Kevin began:

"I adored my older brother. He's tall and handsome, with a sort of golden glow about him. He's also aloof. Has been since my birth, according to Mother. But that didn't keep me from trying to get his attention and his approval. Fat chance.

"When I was almost eleven and he was nearly fourteen, he slipped into my bed late one night, woke me, and whispered that he wanted to get on top of me. I was a fairly adventurous kid, but this seemed scary, even to me. But I obediently lay on my stomach and waited while he pulled down my pajama bottoms and mounted me. How he got it in, I have no idea. I hope he used a little spit. But somehow he did manage to enter. The pain was like nothing I had ever experienced, but I lay there perfectly still and quiet, more frightened of waking our parents than of having my big brother's dick up my ass. As he began to pump me, as quietly as possible, I began to experience that phenomenon known daily all over the world: as the pain decreased, the pleasure increased, until I thought that nothing on Earth could be better.

"He finished and pulled out, unceremoniously. Then he crept back to his bed, leaving me to deal with the aftermath as best I could. I knew there was fluid. I had seen a neighbor ejaculate once. You know, you might like to hear that story, too. Yeah, that's a fun one. Remind me."

"Will do," I said. "How about some more rum?"

"Sure," he answered, and then Kevin continued. "So, there I was with my big brother's load up my ass—for the first time—and I had no idea what to do with it. But I figured it out, like all new challenges. As much as I loved my brother, I always knew I couldn't trust him. But sometimes with our bodies joined in my bed, I would forget. Once I let my guard down enough to whisper, 'I could stay like this forever.' Then, another time, when he pushed his way in too roughly and I balked, he whispered, 'I thought you wanted to do this forever.' There was always an edge, always a distance, no matter how close our bodies were. I definitely wanted more. But I instinctively knew that *more* would always end up being *less* when my brother was part of it.

"We had some daytime encounters too, when both our parents were out. The first time he asked me to blow him, I was willing to do it. But I set ground rules—25¢ was my price, and no more than five forward sucks on the shaft and then I could take a breather and rinse my mouth. He promised not to come in my mouth. Well, he *did* come in my mouth and he *never paid me the quarter!* But it was no worse than I expected. There was always an element of humiliation in our activities. But I preferred that to being ignored.

"I didn't really enjoy having my brother's big dick in my mouth. I just didn't get it at the time. Too young, I suppose. It took me almost ten years to come to full-on dick worship. I met a guy with a particular fondness for being blown. Does that sound like every man you know? But this guy was *really* into it, to the exclusion of practically everything else. He was trim and toned, with nice chest hair, I remember. His dick was a little bit on the small side, but rock hard. At his urging I would go down there and explore. His balls were also small-ish, but very mobile in a large, loose scrotum, so that I could really take one in my mouth and get it close to the back of my throat, where I would have loved to swallow, if it had been possible.

"When I took his dick in my mouth, his body would shiver with pleasure. I realized that I could take the whole thing down my throat, until my upper lip was flattened against his pubic bone. It felt good to take it all. I would stay down there as long as possible. I began to develop new lung capacity. His crotch smelled wonderful, and rubbing my face in his scent was heady stuff. It also gave him an additional charge, so it was win/win. I dated that guy, on and off, for almost a year. It gave me time to not only develop technique—which has served me well in all the years since—but to learn reverence and a deep yearning for dick. I learned that when I served a man well, there would be a reward. That year I went from near-indifference to cum to a passion for it. Somehow, I had never really thought about the taste of cum before. But that year I learned to savor the complex flavors and the luxurious texture, and to crave more.

"I learned to expect different cum flavors depending on what he had been eating. Not just asparagus—we all know that one. But I could tell whether he had been eating a lot of pork, or dairy products, or beef, or green vegetables. I could tell when he had drunk too much beer. I could identify at least a half-dozen different notes when he gave me his essence. I was happy with all of them. That guy taught me a lot. And all it cost me was a few hundred blow-jobs. I'd blow him again—and just about any other man, for that matter—in a heartbeat."

"I think you've earned another splash of rum," Bobby said.

"Why not?" Kevin replied.

I refreshed his glass and then said, "So, how did that go with your brother?"

"Yes, my handsome big brother," he answered. "Those encounters went on for, I don't know, maybe six months? Then he started dating girls and lost interest in me. It did make me wonder if he was just using them, too, or if he really had found a way to give, a way to connect beyond just inserting his dick. I don't know the answer, to this day. I could never figure him out, or my sister-in-law. Much later, it occurred to me that whoever he married, I would always be his first. But let's not go there.

"I was angry. I became *very* angry in my mid-teens. And then I just stuffed it all and became a model high school student. Vice-President of the Senior Class. Year Book. Glee Club. Junior Rotarian. All that shit. It was only after I got away from that horrible town and off to college that I started to access some of those feelings, and then only after a few drinks. I spent a lot of years with the late-night-weepies. It wasn't until I met Sam—did you two know him?"

"I don't think so," Bobby said.

"No, that was a while ago. Sam is the finest man I ever knew. Sam is perfect. He's almost pretty in some kinds of light, and funny-looking in others. But always handsome. He smells like a spring rain. When Sam embraced me, I felt whole. When we made love, he had me totally, like never before—or since. He's also playful. He made me laugh until it hurt.

"It felt like forever. It could have been. Maybe. When Sam got a great job offer in San Francisco, I came within an inch of joining him. But I had worked so hard to find a place for myself in New York, that I just couldn't bear the thought of giving it up. And so, I gave up Sam instead. It was a choice. Was it the right choice? Who the hell knows?

"But my point is that Sam used to tell me that forgiveness is the answer: Never mind the question. Forgive them, and in the doing you automatically forgive *yourself.* And then you can really live. God knows I've tried, through the years, to manage to forgive my brother. I'm not there yet. But closer.

"Look, I'm not complaining. I was present. I was the Party of the Second Part in every action. Nothing happened without my consent. Nothing was forced. I loved it. I wanted more of it. If he had decided that he wanted me for all eternity, I might still be there in that little shit town, serving him. But it does seem just the slightest bit, well, *harsh* that my first lover was largely indifferent.

"What If someone kind and patient had come to me instead? At any age. At *six* I could have loved an adoring man who just wanted to be close to me and shelter me and cherish me. If he also wanted to fuck me three times a day, so much the better, as long as it didn't interfere with school. If he wanted to have several of his *friends* in to fuck me after he was sated, even better, still. I could have done my homework at the same time. It could have been. . .so different."

Bobby said, "You know, I had an early coming-out, too. So, I get it, believe me. But in my case, it wasn't family. I was thirteen when a dirty old man started doing me, so I have some perspective on these things. But family? It's called incest, you know. That seems—more intense. How do you think the experience has shaped you?"

"Oh, I don't know, it's so hard to really talk about these things. But I can tell you this: I've had some great times topping hot guys, and losing my-self totally in the sheer joy of it. Always smaller men, though. If I'm going to be on top, I need to feel bigger, stronger (even when I'm probably not). Dominating a man can be wonderful, if he wants it. And if he doesn't *know* he wants it, it can be even better. I used to love finding short guys—handsome little guys—who didn't know they needed to submit until I came along and showed them what they had been missing.

"There are probably *just* enough hot little guys in the world to satisfy me. Two or three a day would be nice, don't you think? But in my deepest heart, I'm a bottom. I want to take it. I crave being filled. I love the pressure. I love having another man's scent all over me. I want to serve. I want to be used. I want to be an object of pleasure. If that also makes me an object of scorn, then so be it. It feels like love to me. It feels like home.

"I almost forgot to tell you about my neighbor who gave my friend and me a lecture/demonstration on masturbation," Kevin said.

"I think I'm in sensory overload. Could we save that for next time?" I asked.

"Of course."

I wish I could tell you the story about the neighbor and the lecture/demonstration, but I never got to hear it. Kevin was working out of town for a while. When he got back, we spoke on the phone and talked about getting together for dinner. Even in those uncertain times, there didn't seem to be too much urgency about setting a date. Then, a few months later, Kevin called to tell us that he was sick, and that he had decided to move back to his hometown, as much as he dreaded having to go there again. He promised to tell us all about it over brunch.

We got together the week before Kevin left New York. We carefully chose a little restaurant down in the Village with a largely gay clientele. Kevin showed up a little late, looking much too lean. He had skillfully made-up the purplish lesions on his face and neck. Anyone who had not known him before might have overlooked his ashen complexion—anyone, that is, who was unfamiliar with his native hue.

We had a great visit, and really good Eggs Benedict, too. The subject of sex never reared its lovely head, so I never did hear the one about the neighbor and masturbation. "My Aunt Betty called. She said, 'Kevin, dear, ever since your Uncle Jake passed I've been rattling around this big old house by myself. I've been thinking, why don't you come and live here? You're a designer. You can work anywhere. I've got so much space: we can build you a studio if you want. I know this town is not your first choice. It wasn't mine, either. But, what do you say?'

" 'Aunt Betty, I'm sick,' I said. She waited patiently while I hemmed and hawed and then managed to say, 'AIDS.' It was only the second time I'd said it out loud, so I don't know who was more shocked.

" 'Lord have mercy, child. I had no idea. Your mama doesn't tell me shit!' She sputtered a bit, and then said, 'I was hoping you'd come and live here because you *want* to, but maybe you'll come because you *need* to. And that's more important. Just let me know. And your room'll be ready when you are.'

" 'I love you, Aunt Betty,' was all I could manage. If my mother had offered—which she did not—I would have turned her down. Dying in a gutter on Bank Street after being kicked out of my apartment—that would have been preferable. But when

Aunt Betty called, I couldn't say no. I hate going back to my hometown, but at least it's not the house I grew up in, and I don't have to see anyone I don't want to."

Kevin left New York the next week. We spoke on the phone a few times that year. He sounded energized and very much himself. He was working on a new line of belts, I think. They sounded lovely. And then came the call that jangled my quiet afternoon at the word-processor: "Hi, this is Kevin's Aunt Betty. I hate to have to tell you this, but the poor angel died this morning. God bless him. He was ready. I know he loved you two boys, and he'd have wanted you to know."

"We loved him, too. Thanks so much for your call."

"Kevie's mama is making funeral arrangements. I know the family plot is not what he wanted, but she generally gets what *she* wants. Always has, since we were girls. I'll confess I loved that boy more than my own. My husband used to say, 'Betty, don't forget you have younguns of your own!' he'd say. ' I know that, Jake,' I'd tell him, 'but Kevie needs us.' What a sweet boy! You know, he never missed a Mother's Day. Well, it all seems like so long ago, now. I never dreamed I'd be burying that boy. Always thought he'd be burying me! I'll let you go."

"Thanks again for your call," I said. "I know it wasn't easy."

"You boys be good to each other. You never know. I'll hang up now. I think I need a little nap.

I'm suddenly feeling so old! Bye-bye, now." And she hung up. Bobby was out at a rehearsal studio, so I had to process the sorrow alone until dinner time. And then it was good to share the load.

I was outraged about the funeral arrangements. Kevin had left such careful instructions for his cremation. But it was really none of my business, so I let go of it. Mostly. A month later we got together with about twenty of Kevin's other friends for a memorial in Central Park. We spoke, and laughed, and danced, and even sang a little. We released balloons. All of that. I was the one who instigated the tiny fire that was burning brightly when the Park Service guys arrived to put it out. But at least we had given Kevin his pyre. And it was the closest thing to closure that any of us could manage.

Chapter Eleven

Whenever Jay and David called to ask us to dinner, Bobby and I were eager to accept. I didn't have that many friends who cooked for me (then, as now). And these two were not only great fun to be with, but also exceptionally good cooks. David had gone to hotel school, and was working for a food manufacturing organization. Jay worked in PR. They had taken some cooking classes with me, as recreation, and I must say that it was always a relief when I could assign tasks to David's team and know that they would get done. Properly. The boys were also cabaret fans, so our friendship was inevitable.

Jay and David had a large kitchen, by Manhattan standards, and on weekends the two of them would go there together and turn out exceptionally good food that was always pretty, generous, and really delicious. They invited us over on a Saturday evening that summer, in mid-July, I think it was. We dressed as lightly as possible and snagged an air-conditioned cab to take us down to the Village, armed with two bottles of chilled rosé, some bread, and a beautifully ripe reblochon made with a blend of cow, ewe, and goat milk.

The boys were gracious and welcoming, as always. And their basement apartment was so cool it was practically arctic. I was thrilled. They had set a lovely dinner table in the garden, and by the time we headed there we were all coolly comfortable, and the heat of the day had mostly dissipated, especially under the trees in their little oasis.

Dinner began with one of the most glorious dishes ever set before me. The boys made a lobster stew. The real thing—lots of lobster chunks swimming in a bit of milk and cream fortified with lobster essence extracted from the shells by white wine, mostly; an almost nonexistent trace of thyme; a little butter, a pinch of sweet paprika. It was so perfect that I have total sense-memory recall of it. And no memory of the rest of the menu, as a result.

After dessert, as we tucked into the heavenly cheese, I said, "I don't think I ever heard how you two met."

"You've been in New York for a while, I think," Bobby said.

"Eight years now," David said. "I'll let Jay tell the story. He tells a better story than I do."

And Jay began: "It was, I don't know, sort of a leather bar, but with no strict dress code. It's still there, as far as I know. But we left DC two years later, and don't get back very often. The front of the house was maybe unremarkable. A bar. The patrons looked like a cross-section of gay men, some carefully uniformed, others looking more casual. Government workers and the military were regular patrons. A typical DC crowd. They could relax among their own kind, and I never heard of anyone being outed or harassed as a result. So, it resembled any other neighborhood bar except that, on closer look, it was evident that many were wearing the least possible amount of cover. You'll see why.

"In the back was the Men's Room, which might have a variety of activities going on. There might be an S&M performance in progress. There might be a naked guy leaning against the wall, looking as if he was just enjoying a cigarette and just happened to be wearing a series of heavy ball-stretching rings. And in that case, some of the men who entered the room might stop and give Mr. Marlboro a big soul kiss and a serious scrotum tug before proceeding to the urinal. There might be two naked men fucking. Once there was a skinny guy with exceptionally long legs standing on the sink while a beefy biker type rimmed him. I didn't wash my hands that time, for fear of breaking the spell. There might be a naked guy stretched out in the urinal waiting to receive all offerings. In fact, the long, galvanized urinal could accommodate as many as four supplicants, so one could choose which boy to shower. It was always fun to go into the Men's to pee at the Falcon. There was always a feeling that anything might happen.

"But the back deck was the heart of the club, for six months of the year, anyway. It was wall-to-wall men, packed in together. Come to think of it, I never tried to go there in the winter, did you?"

"No," David said, "But I suspect the concentration of men conserves body heat."

"I have a feeling there was enough concentrated body heat on that deck for all but blizzard conditions," Jay said. "The guys were mostly shirtless. What they might be wearing below—or packing below--was a matter to be discovered. The whole idea was to wend one's way ever-so-slowly through the crowd, stopping to explore anyone of interest. The Hajj, if wasn't. But it was such a friendly place that the worst rebuff you could receive from an uninterested hottie was a smile and a slight "no" shake of the head.

"A gentle grope, a kiss, a nipple tweak, a caress—these were generally tolerated by all. No one was there to swan. No one was there to be worshiped from a distance. No one was saving himself for Mr. Right. It was about community. You could stay upright and let your fingers roam. You could dip down below the surface and find all sorts of things to do with your hands and your tongue. Or you could just wait and let things come to you. It might be a kiss. It might be a blowjob from an invisible stranger. Or it might be a big ol' dick knocking at the back door. The scene was fraught with possibilities.

"I was there one summer night when there was a beautiful guy in the middle of the crowd, with a truly exquisite face. He was radiant, like Christ in a low-budget picture, and he was being embraced from behind by a huge leather daddy. By the ecstatic look on the beauty's face, it was clear that he was receiving something important back there. David and I—who had never met—both spotted him at the same instant, and both decided to go down for a better look. We met on opposite sides of the beauty's equally beautiful penis—which was not otherwise engaged. We had to accept that our arrivals were simultaneous, and so we shared the honors. We took turns blowing him and nuzzling his gorgeous balls. We gave up all territoriality and just shared the bounty as equally as possible. When the beauty blew his load, David happened to be the lucky recipient. He waited for every possible drop. And then he turned to me and kissed me deeply, sharing the gift he had just received. We both stood and continued our sloppy kisses, an ethereally beautiful man's cum smeared all over our faces. 'Let's go to my place' I said.

" 'I'll bet my place is closer,' David said. And so it was, only two blocks away. We ran most of the way, and then fell into his bed, out of breath but invigorated. And then we spent the next few hours laughing, and kissing, and fucking. And we've been doing it ever since. Next week it'll be ten years, and we've never slept a night apart in all that time."

〰

We had Jay over for dinner twice the year after David died. Jay's health was fairly okay, then. He was a little too thin, but otherwise not in bad shape. He just had lost all joy in his life, and he couldn't figure out a way to get it back. Bobby and I felt rather useless. No matter how much our love for Jay increased—and we truly focused all the affection we had felt for the two of them on Jay alone—it seemed almost irrelevant.

I tried to cook tempting, comforting food, as I did for all my sick friends. At one dinner I remember I made a big baked pasta extravaganza that contained more vegetables than Eve's garden. And I even made *crème brûlée* for dessert. Jay ate it, and he thanked me for it. But I sensed that nothing could taste great to him without David at his side to share it.

The following year, Jay had to give up the Village apartment with the wonderful kitchen and the garden and twelve years of exquisite memories. By that point he was resigned, and weak, and willing

113

to shift worlds from a joyous place of comfort and love to a nearly-bare little room that a charity had found for him.

I visited Jay two or three times at his new digs. Or, I should say, I visited what was left of him. I don't do a very good Florence Nightingale, but I made the effort. And each time, what clutched at my throat, as I watched my friend dying, was seeing the only souvenirs that he brought from his old life, his *real* life, and put on the night table beside his bed—David's little Teddy bear with the chef's hat, sitting on top of a well-thumbed copy of *MASTERING THE ART OF FRENCH COOKING, VOLUME ONE.*

Chapter Twelve

I hope you'll remember that I promised to tell you more about Josh Walker. I don't have the space for *ALL ABOUT JOSH*, nor the insight, nor the information. But I want to share what little I have. This Joshua may not have fit the battle of Jericho, but he done fit a whole lot of other battles in order to get himself to New York: dance training, voice training, and acting classes. And he arrived ready to work.

Josh Walker was hot stuff. Bobby was very impressed when he came to audition for a revue that was being planned for a theater company that had an excellent track record of transfers to Broadway. That show was staged the fall before, I think. Surely that's why we thought to invite them to our New Year's Day do.

The revue was maybe smallish, but then, who knows where these things might go? Josh was anything but small: He had a big, rich baritone, and exceptionally long legs that he could throw over his head with effortless ease. Or at least he made it look that way. Josh was young, pretty, talented, winning, and limber. So, if one needed to cast the hot young black character who sings and dances, then one would do well to pay close attention to this find.

Josh got the part, and his availability matched the limited run that had been planned. So it was all set. There were other cast members, of course. Four women, as I remember. The show celebrated the work of a famous female lyricist, who did indeed write some exceptionally fine songs for women. And the exceptionally fine lyrics she contributed to songs that might be especially well-suited to *men* were assigned to Josh. More or less.

It was a good show. The songs were mostly pure gold, and the performers were delightful. For ages now I've been saying, *Actors, God bless 'em!*, meaning, *Actors, as a class of people, are so willing and fearless that they just get out there and do it, no matter what!* So, even if the stage is too small, or the costumes are not quite optimal, or the acoustics or the sound system are challenging, or even if they are not so happy with their lighting, they just do it! Every time! Bobby normally fell in love with every collaborator, and this show was no exception. But some more than others, of course.

Josh was not only handsome and talented, but he had the good fortune to find his soul-mate early on. We're not all so lucky, as I'm sure you know. But Josh found his kindred spirit in the remarkable guise of Johnny Barnett. I'll confess that I've had more than my fair share of fantasies about being a fly on the wall in the same room where the two of them were making love. Being a *human* in the same *bed* with them would have been even nicer, but never mind. The guys were both so stunning that it seemed almost beside the point that they were also both charming, talented, and very friendly. I liked them, both, very much. But, maybe, Josh, a little more.

Johnny was about ten years older than Josh and was not only an excellent dancer but also a talented choreographer. He did some shows that were well received in New York, and around the country, too. Johnny had two young children, from a previous relationship, who lived with him and Josh, in a neat house in a small city in New Jersey. Within commuting distance, of course. I never asked them, "Why New Jersey?" but I suspect they wanted to establish a home for the kids away from the bustle of city—and show biz—life.

Johnny worked a lot, and traveled a lot, so Josh did a *whole* lot of Mr. Mom. I'm sure he did it really well, because the kids obviously adored him, and seemed to thrive in that home setting. I only visited once. The children—a boy and a girl, ages ten and nine—were bouncing around the living room, as children do, until a neighboring mom arrived to collect them for what we now call a "play date." Josh's kids piled into the station-wagon with the neighbor kids, and off they all went for a summer adventure.

Josh made a pot of tea—the Southern one flavored with sweet spice and orange peel—and I brought some cheese wafers with ground pecans that were a particular favorite from my Southern childhood. Not that my mother baked them, but friends' mothers did. Baking always takes me back to the *best* of the past. The warmth of the kitchen and the aromas from the oven can almost erase the hurts. Almost.

Josh had some hurts of his own, of course. "My grandmother used to bake these same cheese wafers," he said. "I could swear it's her recipe. She baked them for the family she worked for, and she baked just enough extra that she could leave a few for us. I'll never forget watching her in her spotless little kitchen chopping the pecans until they were as fine as cornmeal, then mixing the dough in a big old earthenware bowl. She was particularly careful about adding the perfect pinch of cayenne—just enough to create a little excitement, but not so much that the white ladies would blush."

"When the texture was right—and I think I'd recognize it, to this day—she scooped the dough out onto sheets of wax paper and rolled them up into logs. They were always exactly one-inch in diameter. Her eye would have been sufficient, but she also took a ruler to each roll, just to assure herself that they were perfect. Twenty-four-hours to cool and cure, and then—slice and bake."

"I had to do a little research," I said, "but I found an old recipe in a facsimile cookbook—*Southern Receipts*, that sort of thing. This, and a buttermilk pie, and an okra casserole felt just right to me. And of course we all know who did the cooking for the grand Southern ladies who wrote those books."

"My grandmother!"

"Exactly!" I said. "It took me a really long time to figure that all out. It wasn't until I fell in love with New Orleans and creole cooking that I started to sort of get it—that black cooks had been shaping the cuisine over two centuries. It's still the best cooking in the US, I'm sure. Louisiana, especially, but the rest of the South, too. And, hey, let's hear it for your ancestors in the Low Country!"

"I thought South Carolina would kill me," Josh said, "and it might have, if I'd stayed."

"Amen, Brother!," I said. I felt *really* silly about my response, and yet *my* escape from *North* Carolina felt just as critical as *his* escape, at that moment. "It just sucked the wind out of me. Daily," I said. And I sort of grabbed his free hand that wasn't pouring tea and clutched it. Josh didn't seem to mind. We sat quietly for a bit, savoring our very Southern tea and our very Southern cheese wafers.

.   "You two seem very happy together," Josh said. "Bobby's from?

"Detroit."

"Ouch! That couldn't have been easy, either," he said.

"No, I'm sure it wasn't. But, how many towns are dying to nurture gifted gay boys?" I asked.

"Not mine, I can assure you," Josh said. "There was only one other person in that town I loved, aside from my grandmother. And my sister, of course. But, unfortunately, the boy I fell in love with was the son and heir in the family Grandma worked for. Michael. Michael Wainwright. We were the same age, but we went to separate schools, of course, so we would never have met except that Grandma needed me to help her, sometimes, take food and sewing she had been working on up to the 'big house.'

"It was a nice house, actually. Large, but not too fancy. The Wainwrights made their money in trade—and not by cheating 'poor niggers' out of their wages, as some other families did. They were not invested in that 'Southern aristocracy' bullshit. They just wanted to run a good business and live a comfortable life, and they could afford to do it. My grandmother was a *very* proud woman. She was *nobody's* girl. She was always Mrs. Walker. Mrs. Wainwright, and everyone else in the household, called my grandmother Mrs. Walker, and it would

119

not have occurred to any of them to do otherwise. And I think my grandmother would have relocated if there had ever been a breach of etiquette.

"Michael was not blond, exactly. The Wainwrights didn't have that inbred Southern thing going on. He was just handsome."

"Josh, I have to tell you," I said. "I have a friend who grew up in Waycross, Georgia. He's great looking. He's also hot, but let's not go there. Anyway, I have to go back to my hometown now and then—as little as possible—and whenever I see a good-looking man—which is not that often—I think, 'Oh, he looks *so* much like James.' And then one day it occurred to me that there is only one kind of handsome white boy in the South. And he looks like a Confederate lieutenant."

"Exactly! And they *are* pretty, aren't they?"

"Indeed."

"Michael would ask me to help him with projects on the grounds. And in the summer we would take off our shirts when we were building a stone wall or chopping wood or something. I knew he was just as attracted to me as I was to him, all sweaty and macho. But I would never have touched him if he hadn't made the first move. We were in a remote part of the property, down by the pond, when he suggested that we take a swim to cool off. I agreed, of course. I waited for him to strip down to bare, and then I did the same.

"We ran into the water and then laughed and splashed each other, as boys do. We were both seventeen that summer. Seventeen would be a wonderful age if it weren't so painful, don't you think?" Josh sipped his tea and picked at some imaginary lint on the sofa. And then he resumed:

"Michael grabbed my head and pushed me underwater, and then I returned the favor, and then we were locked in a sort of wrestling embrace, and then he kissed me. Michael Wainwright kissed me full on the lips, and held me close, and pressed his boner right up against me. I was orgasmic—well, before long. We both were. We clutched each other in that silly old pond way out behind his house, and we made love.

"I had never had sex with another boy before. I don't know about Michael. But sure as shit I can tell you that what we two did that summer was *make love*. As often as possible. Wherever we could. Whenever we could find a little space and time to be alone. He never invited me up to his bedroom. That would have been too obvious. That would have been a violation of protocol. But it was a big place, and there were some almost remote parts, like the old ice house, and the pond, of course.

"It was fall of our senior year in high school, and still the weather was mostly hot, and still we would meet up, especially on Saturdays. We met that day in an old shed—an old carriage house. He held me so gently, and kissed me so tenderly, that I said, 'Michael, I love you.'

"He pushed me away, and said, 'What do you mean, Josh. You love me? You're out of your fucking mind! Do you want to see me in jail and you swinging from a tree? No, this is not happening. Out! Out of here! I don't ever want to see you again as long as I live.'

" 'Michael, please!"

" 'No! Out!'

" 'Michael!'

121

"And then he punched me so hard that I fell back on the dirt floor of that old carriage house, the same floor that had been carefully compacted by generations of slaves, maybe even some of my ancestors. Who the fuck knows. My nose started to bleed, generously. Michael came over to me, knelt down, and kissed me deeply, blood and all. And then he helped me up and then pretty much pushed me out the door and in the direction of my grandmother's house.

"Grandma knew what was going on, of course. She was a smart old bird. She said nothing when I came stumbling into her house and headed to the bathroom to rinse off the residue of the last half hour. But then she knocked softly on the bathroom door. When I opened it, she was standing there with a little towel and some ice-cubes she had freed from the old metal ice-cube tray in her Kelvinator. She helped me ice down my nose and the bags that were forming under my eyes.

"I had no intention of explaining what had happened, and she never asked for an explanation. She asked nothing. But after the bleeding had stopped and my face had begun to stabilize, she said to me, very quietly, 'It's their way.' And that was it. End of story.

"I thought I'd die if I couldn't have Michael. But, you know what? I didn't. And then that winter Mr. Wainwright helped me get a scholarship to an arts school in Columbia, and I was out of there. And then I got to New York as fast as I could. Did I ever tell you, I auditioned for Johnny my first month in town, like, maybe my third audition? And he said, 'You've got the part, and a whole lot more if you want it.'

"And I said, 'Yes, I'll take it!' And here we are, six years later, pillars of society!"

"You two are my favorite suburban couple, hands down," I said. "And I want to thank you for your most gracious welcome," I said in my creepiest laid-on Southern manners. And then it was time to leave.

I gathered up my stuff, and as I was saying good-bye, I gave Josh a big hug and planted a big kiss on his beautiful mouth. He kissed me back, to my surprise. I felt those stirrings low in the torso. And I could swear that Josh was stirring, too. And any stirring at all from Josh would certainly be unmistakable, not to mention much more impressive than mine. Yes, he was stirring. I'm certain of it. Had it been later in the day, and after a cocktail or two, I'm sure I would have jumped him. He, me? Probably not. But it was a quiet summer afternoon, and he needed to start dinner for the kids, who would be home in a few hours. And I needed to head to the bus stop for the trip home to my own love nest. And that was our last meeting.

📖

The kids were mid-teens when the guys got sick—first Johnny, and then Josh. I was shocked by the news, even though I should have been past shock by that point. I know it sounds like I think it's all about me, but, after all, what other filter do I have for sifting information? I was especially horrified by the idea of the future the kids were facing. I knew they had gotten off to a rough start with their not-so-stable mother. And that they had found a loving home with their two daddies. And now?

Josh had a sister the two kids knew and loved. "Aunt Rebecca" was like a slightly softer-looking version of Josh, nearly as tall, and every bit as beautiful. I only met her once, at the opening-night party after the revue that Josh did with Bobby. And yet I've pinned my hopes for those hapless kids squarely on her very lovely, very broad shoulders. In my fantasy, Rebecca stepped right up and took over their guardianship. It's only conjecture, but anything less would simply be unthinkable.

Chapter Thirteen

The first week in August, we went to a memorial for a young guy Bobby had been working with, up until about six months before. Nathaniel Randolph was the rather grandiose name he chose for himself. And in that act of creation, little Jimmy Jones transformed himself from a runty orphan of no significance into a new, talented, lissome, even mysterious creature.

Nate made his way to New York—as people who reinvent themselves so often do—found Bobby, and asked him for coaching and arrangements. Bobby judged him to be attractive and engaging, and he agreed to hear Nate sing. I also have to mention that Nate appeared to be packing an endowment so impressive that it tested the ability of his jeans to contain it. So, of course, that only added to his physical appeal.

Nate came by the apartment the next afternoon to audition. I happened to be home, so I got to hear (from the kitchen) while he sang a few standards. I thought he sounded pretty good. Bobby was satisfied that Nate had enough talent and drive to get work. Nate also seemed to wear well. Some people can make a good first impression, only to seem less attractive and less winning at the next meeting.

But Nate was solidly himself. Which is always a good thing.

This was the summer of 1984, I think, and Nate had met a club owner who was willing to give him a few nights—Tuesdays in January. So, in about four months' time he had to be ready with a new cabaret show. He asked Bobby about doing a one-composer evening. Nate had always been drawn to Mort Harriman's songs. And the fact that Bobby and Mort were old friends did no harm.

Bobby and Nate went to work on the show, deciding on material, planning arrangements and medleys—all that nightclub stuff. I've never understood quite how it's done, but I can certainly feel it when it's right, and, especially, when it's wrong. You don't need to know too much about this process, just that Nate came by whenever Bobby had a free afternoon. And they created a show.

We also had Nate over for dinner a few times that fall. He really was very cute, and our other friends enjoyed spending time with him. Even Geoffrey seemed kinder and more—pleasant—when Nate was around. And that was certainly a plus. One night in November, I threw together a quick supper for a friend of Bobby's who had also become a friend of mine—Anita Arlen She was going on tour and would be gone for a year. It was our last chance to see her before her travel day.

Fall is a great time of year to cook, and I ran out to the market and scooped up a big loin of pork and winter squashes to roast, and apples and pears to serve with ripened cheeses. Some Brussels sprouts to go with the roast. And a little smoked salmon to start. Easy stuff. Festive, too. I was feeling it.

We had decided on six for dinner—Nate, Geoff, Anita and her lover, Alice, and the two of us. It felt like a good mix, and indeed it was. We ate well, and drank well, and everyone was very well-behaved. Even Geoff. He insulted no one. Even when we had gotten into the after-dinner drinks, there was harmony. Alice was a hoot, as it happened, and she had me in stitches all evening. It's always a treat to meet new people who are warm and funny. When the ladies said their good-nights and we wished Anita a wonderful tour, I was feeling the contentment that hosts feel when they have cared for their guests properly. It's a lovely feeling, when things go right. They don't always.

I remembered the first time Anita came to the house for dinner, early-on in my life with Bobby. As she was leaving, she gave me a fierce hug, and said, very quietly, as she spun me around out of everyone-else's earshot, "I think you two are wonderful together. I've never seen Bobby happier. But just know that if you hurt him, I'll cut your balls off." I assured her that I had no intention of doing anything hurtful, and she released her grip on my arm. I could easily imagine how that grip would feel on other body parts.

But *this* evening, as Anita thanked me for dinner, and for arranging to get us all together before her tour, she was warm as toast. I assured Anita that we would try to be good friends to Alice while she was away—dinners and phone calls, that sort of thing. It was a promise I would be happy to keep.

After Anita and Alice headed home—rather early because of Anita's morning departure—we boys headed to the living room for a visit. The subject of

127

HIV came up, as it so often did in those days. And Nate mentioned, almost in passing, that he was positive. No one expressed shock, of course. A very pleasant, very talented, very pretty young man mentioned that he had been served a death sentence. And no one reacted. Because it would have been cruel, *and* because it had become quotidian.

I fussed with bottles and glasses. Geoff was always happy to accept a splash of Crown Royal. You know already what Bobby and I drank. Nate was not really drinking at all, except for toying with half a glass of red with dinner. But he accepted a tiny glass of Chartreuse. As I stepped over to his chair to hand it to him, I looked down at his lovely little body and his lovely big crotch. As he looked up at me and smiled a thank-you, I wondered how hearts can handle these things—his heart, or mine, for that matter.

Geoff launched into a story about some indignity he had recently suffered on the subway. We were all sympathetic. And then I said, "Nate, I don't really know you very well. What's your story? If you don't mind my asking."

"No, not at all," Nate said. "There's not that much to tell. I headed to LA when I was twenty. One night my second week I met this hot guy in a club in West Hollywood. He took me home to a fabulous house in the hills above Sunset—you know the kind, lots of space, low furniture, big swimming pool. The sex was great, and the next morning he asked me to stay to lunch. That's when I realized he was Victor Deloro, the fashion designer. He wanted me to stick around, and I did. I didn't own anything much at the time, so he took me clothes shopping on Rodeo Drive. We were having a good time, and we had hot sex at least twice a day.

"I was really enjoying myself, but also feeling as if my life had stalled. But Victor was good about helping me develop. He found me a great vocal coach, and made it a point to take me to the best places to see and be seen. I had no illusions about being the first young thing on his arm, but I was having too much fun to complain about anything. About six months into our relationship, I happened to open his medicine cabinet to find some aspirin, because I didn't have any in mine. And there was a huge collection of drugs with names I couldn't pronounce. I gave up the search for aspirin, and tried to take a little nap instead, to cure my headache.

"I didn't want to see it, but it gradually became clear that not only was Victor using all the usual Hollywood uppers and downers and euphorics, but he also had some health issues that were being treated—not very successfully—with powerful prescription drugs. And as he had more and more 'bad colds' and other ailments, I had to accept that he was in what I'd now call the pre-AIDS state. And we had been having unprotected sex for months! When I confronted him, he refused to discuss it, and so I moved out—back to my old rooming house in West Hollywood.

I was scared shitless, but there wasn't so much I could do, besides getting an HIV test, just to be certain. Not that I wasn't already. But the confirmation gave it another layer of reality. I didn't exactly become a monk. I still went out occasionally. One night I was at a club when Victor swept in with his new boy. And before long the new boy was flirting with me. 'Victor tells me you have a really big dick. Let's go out back.' This kid wanted me to screw him without a condom!

"I said to myself, 'Fuck this!' And the next morning I went out and got myself a job on a cruise ship. Anything to get out of that town. It was an Alaska run. The scenery was beautiful; the passengers, not so much. We kids performed a revue of pop standards in various lounges around the ship. It was fine. The music was nice. I love to sing. It was fine. But I was so terrified that I was drinking—*a lot*—to try to control the terror.

"I woke up early one morning when a deck steward roused me. And I realized that I had no idea what I had done the night before, no idea who I had done it with, and no idea how I had ended up on that deck chair. And I decided there had to be a better way.

"I went to an AA meeting on-board that afternoon. And then I started to focus on changing my life. The cruise job would be over in another month, and New York felt right. I always loved it. I grew up in New Jersey, you know."

"No, I didn't," I said.

"Plainfield. Couldn't wait to get out. But I have adoptive parents. They're nice people. And they love me."

"You'd be, oh, so easy to love," I said, knowing that I was speaking to a group that would be sure to get any Cole Porter reference.

As we were undressing for bed that night, Bobby turned to me and gave me a hug, and I realized that he was crying. "It's just so terribly unfair," he said, "that Nate has to go through this."

"I know, Sweetie," I said. What else is there to say?

Nate's cabaret show went really well. He was fun, and sexy, and musical, and smart; sometimes a little dangerous, but always engaging—like Mort Harriman's songs. Mort came to opening night, as did the cabaret critic for *The New York Times*. Without blowing Bobby's horn too loudly, I must say that his collaboration not only added artistic value (as always) but also a level of clout that young performers struggle to find. Bobby had a good time, and he was perfectly willing to try it again.

There might have been a next project. They talked about it. They even decided to try the one-composer angle again. I don't remember who it was. But Bobby got busy, and Nate was in a revue in the Village that became fairly popular, and when it was time to get back to collaboration, Nate's health started to fail.

Bobby took it worse than I did. Much worse. I knew Bobby had a crush on Nate that went beyond friendship and their artistic bonds. I respected it. Hey, glass houses, and all. But when the reality of Nate's condition began to intrude on our lives, Bobby became pretty much what we used to call inconsolable. I'm not saying that he drew the shades and took to his bed with a little bottle of aromatic spirits of ammonia. It's just that he was in pain. And there was no relief for the pain that I could offer.

As Nate lay dying, I was visiting him one afternoon when the couple who had raised him, the Joneses, told him that his birth mother had named him Nathaniel. And so they marveled at his choice

of names, considering that he could not possibly
have known.

"I always said that was my name," I heard him
say, more or less, as he slipped into a nap. Or perhaps it was a fever- or drug-induced lapse. They
were all very much the same at that point. That
was the last time I saw Nate. Bobby went once
more that last week. And then what was left of
Nate's exquisite little body was spent.

And there we were at another memorial. It was
attended by a handful of young gypsies and assorted cabaret people, and a few dozen of Nate's AA
friends. The Joneses, of course. Even Mort Harriman showed up, which was a very kind gesture. I
was only maybe half present, at that point. I guess
that's about how I processed much of the loss that
decade. Have I revisited it and actually experienced
it this time? At this late date? Couldn't I just avoid
it for another decade or two? Apparently not.

Chapter Fourteen

The Hotel Amagansett has had a place in New York history for nearly a century. Bobby and Mary did mostly two engagements a year in the Walnut Room in the mid-'80s. They introduced some of their most successful shows—that became some of their most collectible albums—in that dark-paneled, clubby bastion of old, masculine privilege.

But the Amagansett has a lighter side as well—the Orchid Room. It's more welcoming—an extension of the lobby, really. That's where the famous Round Table wits lunched, as did a few generations of privileged women. And at dinner time, it was considered a perfect venue for nervous young would-be grooms to pop the question.

The Orchid Room also had perhaps the most charming maître d' in New York. Sean LeFevre was tall and lean, and cut a dashing figure in his hotel livery. He could be as imperious as the next gate-keeper, but he also had a kindness and generosity about him that was quite lovely. I know he was patient with tourists and young people who were just trying to have a nice experience. I never heard it said that he was rude to anyone, and I feel quite certain that he never was.

One evening when I went to the Walnut Room to hear Mary and Bobby, I stopped by the Orchid Room and invited Sean to dinner. He was off on

Monday nights—as was Bobby—so that worked out well. It was September, and there was still a good supply of Southern seafood in the market. So I decided to make my favorite gumbo—crab and shrimp with sausages, finished with filé powder.

I had learned to make it five years before from a New Orleans chef whose very hot son offered me his father's help. This particular gumbo has everything going for it, as far as I'm concerned: It's rich and spicy, smoky, deeply flavored with seafood—the perfect expression of the urban creole chef's art worked on the simple ingredients of Acadian country. Heavenly. And since Sean was from New Orleans, I sensed that he would appreciate it. And if I made a big pot, then there would be more for Bobby and me the next day. Or two.

On Monday afternoon I steamed the crabs and peeled the shrimp. When the crabs were just cool enough to handle, I pulled off the top shells and scooped out the tomalley and roe, setting them aside for later. The shells went back into the pot with the shrimp shells and a few aromatics and some white wine to simmer along for a rich stock. All I had to do with the crab bodies was to remove and discard the gills and stomachs, and then snap the bodies in half. They would go into the soup just like that, and the flavor from those shells would lend extraordinary savor.

Once I had all the vegetables chopped, then I could start the roux. It's a careful stirring process, waiting patiently until the roux is chocolate-colored but not burned, and then in go the veggies. The burst of steam that rises from the pot as the aromatics are stirred into the dangerously-hot roux is so fragrant, that it makes the entire process worthwhile. Even if I didn't get to taste the finished product, it would still be satisfying. But, fortunately, I get to do both.

That September afternoon, I puttered along with my gumbo, and also prepared the rice and the rest of the meal: I roasted two chickens and trimmed some okra pods to steam at the last minute. We would then have a salad with beefsteak tomatoes—the Jerseys were quite good that year. And so were the figs, so I had gotten two baskets of them and a ripened triple-crème cheese. We were all set.

Sean arrived, fashionably late, with a lovely bouquet of flowers. Scooter was sometimes skittish about tall men. Sean must have grown up around small dogs, because he knew how to get down to Scooter's level for the initial sizing-up. And then Scooter became devoted to Sean, and scarcely left his side all evening.

Dinner was delicious. Sean said he loved the gumbo, and he asked for seconds. I was pleased. "How did you get to New York?" I asked him, over dessert.

"It was a little round-about. I love New Orleans, but I just don't want to actually *live* there anymore. New York seemed scary. I had restaurant experience, so I was able to get a job in Chicago. And off I went."

"I was in Chicago, too. Early '70s. That's where Bobby and I met," I said.

"*Mid-*'70s for me," Sean said. "So I guess that's how we missed each other. I like Chicago. I was there for maybe three years. But when there was an opening at the Amagansett, I was out of Chicago like a shot."

I suggested coffee in the living room, and I also poured cognacs all around. We sat and sighed a little over our full bellies. Scooter settled in between Sean's feet. Bobby asked about the hotel. I knew that it was family-owned. "How are the Brightleys to work for?" he asked Sean.

"Delightful," Sean replied. "They couldn't be more supportive."

"They've always been very polite to me, but as often as Mary and I play the Walnut Room, we're still outsiders—not part of the hotel family, like you are."

"They're not exactly warm and fuzzy, as you know, but both Mr. and Mrs. are always fair and respectful. We don't see the kids very often, but when they do show up they're very pleasant. It's the best business environment I've worked in," Sean said.

"Glad to hear it," Bobby said.

"I want to hear more about Chicago," I said.

"Poor Sean," Bobby said. "Once he's on the scent, I doubt you can shake him."

"Oh, that's okay. Actually, I do have a story, and if you'll pour me another cognac I suspect I can tell it."

"It's a deal," I said, and poured.

Sean began: "My first year in Chicago, I was working as a waiter in a large hotel on Lake Shore Drive. There was a restaurant, plus private dining rooms and room service. A lot going on, all catered from one big kitchen. I worked dinners in the restaurant several nights a week, and also some lunches. I'll never forget one Monday morning when I dragged myself out of bed just in time to make the lunch shift, and discovered that my dick was weeping that unmistakable greenish discharge that we all knew in those days was gonorrhea. Or at least, we *hoped* that it was gonorrhea and not something worse.

"I tried to do the right thing. I called the supervisor and told him that I couldn't make it to work. He insisted that I *had* to make it in, that there was no one else to work the shift. So, I showered, dressed, packed my shorts with tissues, and went to work. I was careful to wash my hands often and avoid handling the food, so I was an exemplary employee that day. But it was an icky experience, and I was thrilled when I could break out and head to the clinic where I knew there would be penicillin.

"But the story I want to tell, from that time, is about one of the waiters I saw only occasionally. He worked private events and room service, I guess. I know he had a regular job as well; I just can't remember what it was. We never shared a shift in the dining room. Mostly I saw him afternoons after I had finished lunch. Abraham was average height, dark-skinned, trim, always neatly groomed and uniformed, with a ready smile, a nice round butt, and a very pleasant way about him. He also had a serious crush on me.

"Now, I was cute enough, then, I suppose. . ."

"And now," I said.

"Well, thanks. I'm not so sure. But anyway, Abe had it bad. I had no idea how to handle it. I liked him, but I didn't *like* him. I smiled and exchanged pleasantries when we ran into each other. And when he asked me out, I found ways to put him off. Politely. Always politely. Because, who knows? I should mention that he had a best friend and co-worker named Jerry, who was a skinny little

fortyish white boy who obviously resented me and
made no attempt to hide it.

"That would have been the end of the story, except that one Saturday, after lunch, when I had the
rest of the weekend off, for some reason or other,
Abe happened to be finishing up his shift, too. I
was feeling blue, for some reason I don't really remember. *Very* blue. Mood indigo, we're talking
about. And Abe was there, his usual pleasant self,
with a suggestion that we might get together.

"And then I said to him something like this:
'Abe, you're a really nice guy. And I really need
that. I would love to go home with you, and spend
the rest of the weekend with you, but it has to be
just this one time. If you're okay with that, then
let's go to your place.'

"Abe agreed to the one-time-only clause, and off
we went. Abe's apartment was nice enough, I
think. We spent most of the time in his bed. He
coddled me, and fucked me, and fed me. He was
warm, and enveloping. And then Sunday night, I
headed home.

"Surely, Abe hoped that our time together would
change my mind, that I would feel the attraction
that he felt. But, of course, it doesn't work that
way. I was grateful because he had offered me
comfort when I felt desperately lonely. He was willing to take a chance on something more, when I
only offered very little. We both kept to our bar-
gain.

"The rest of the story is that I never saw Abe
again. He stopped working those shifts that had
overlapped mine. He just disappeared. His friend
Jerry would shoot dagger-glances at me. And then,
finally, when it was obvious that Abe was avoiding

the hotel, Jerry deigned to tell me something like, 'You broke his heart, and now he won't come back here, because he can't bear to see you again!'

"Now, there's a family story about my grandfather (a jilted maiden, a suicide), but no one in my generation—least of all little me—has inspired that kind of drama. I doubt that Abe pined away for years for lack of me, but I can't say. I might have been willing to just let the whole thing go and chalk it up to youth. We've all dated attractive men and then decided, no, this is not working. Except that, you see, there was a disturbing truth underneath. It's very hard for me to admit this, and I couldn't do it if I hadn't had a few drinks:

"I knew, at the time, somewhere just below the surface, not quite up front, that I was incapable of having a black lover. No matter how many big black dicks I took up my ass, and how many more I hoped to take in the future, I just could not wrap my brain around the concept of sharing my life with a black man.

"Abe was *not* the man for me, clearly, and if I had spent more time with him, I might have missed out on everything that New York has to offer. And I love my life here. But as long as I live, I'll always be haunted by questions about how race works itself into our lives, even when we can't see the specter, even when we think we've left the old ways behind."

Sean fell silent, and then petted Scooter, who was still at his feet, and who was grateful for the attention, as always. *I* was grateful for Sean's honesty, and told him so. And I felt a little squirm at the bottom of my own Southern heart, wondering where *I* was in the evolutionary chain. Sean thanked me for dinner, and told me that my gumbo made him home-sick.

Scooter needed a walk, and so I clipped on his leash so the two of us could walk Sean to First Avenue, where there were always cabs. Even after midnight. Neither Scooter nor I really wanted to let him go, but even the best evenings must wind down.

Once Scooter and I returned from reluctantly sending Sean on his way home, Bobby and I organized the apartment, a bit. Just enough so that we could face the kitchen in the morning. I was more *laissez-faire*—then as now—and Bobby was more *let's get this mess out of the way.* As we washed and dried some glassware and put it away, Bobby said, "What a lovely man!"

"Yes," I said. "And Scooter agrees."

"And we all know Scooter has impeccable taste. He lives with us, after all." And so he did.

It was about two years later we learned that Sean was sick. He was one of the guys who developed encephalitis while he still looked the picture of health. Well, nearly. And within a week or two he was dead. The horror of it all was difficult to accept. I never knew whether to feel that the universe was offering tender mercies to the boys who went fast—sparing them the pain of extended wasting and suffering—or whether they were even more cruelly victimized than the ones who had some time to learn to accept their fate.

Sean's mother and his little brother—who was also gay—came from New Orleans for the funeral.

The Brightley's put them up at the hotel, and that was very generous of them. The situation was terrible enough, but the night after Sean's funeral, the brother picked up some rough trade, apparently, and brought him back to the hotel. And the hustler murdered him, right there in his bed in his room at the Amagansett. Shoved his head between the slats in the headboard and crushed his skull, or snapped his spinal column, or who-the-fuck-knows how these things can be.

How fantastical is that? And yet it happened. The unimaginable suffering of Sean's mother—who came to New York to bury a son and ended up burying two—has haunted me all these years. I've never found tools for processing even the idea of it, much less the reality of the loss. I don't see how anyone could.

Chapter Fifteen

Bobby decided to do a Cole Porter show in Boston that fall. The timing looked good: only a month out-of-town, and he would definitely be home for Thanksgiving. I liked Boston when I was there once before. And I also knew that John lived there. John Alegria, the handsome boy I had a crush on in the summer of '76, in Provincetown. *Wouldn't it be fun to see John again?* I thought. Is that what made me decide to accompany Bobby to Boston? No, not really; but it helped. I made plans to travel with Bobby and then stay for a week, mostly to help him get settled into the furnished apartment that would be his home for the next month.

The apartment was on the west end of town, in a student section that backs onto Fenway Park, just below Back Bay. We quickly fell into a routine. The T stop was nearby, and it was a straight shot to the theater district (such as it is). While Bobby was working, I would go to a big discount store for sheets and towels, and a few little things for the kitchen and bath. After his rehearsals we would stop for supper at one of the little cafés on Newbury Street, often with some of the cast members. And then it was back to the apartment for late-night TV. The apartment had a sleeping loft, and Bobby took to it, to my surprise. I thought he would hate climbing the ladder and crawling into a bed without much headroom. It turned out that I was the one who would have been happier sleeping on the couch. But, of course, I joined him each night in his little hippie loft adventure.

The second day, I phoned John. He sounded glad to hear from me. We made date for lunch in two days. I was looking forward to seeing John again, of course. It seemed a perfect sort of meeting. Autumnal. Warm, but with a trace of winter in it. I had already noticed that—come fall— sundown is earlier in Boston than in New York. And I was glad that we had decided on a midday meeting. It seemed to require full sunlight.

I dressed with a little extra care the morning of our luncheon. I also studied my face in the mirror, wondering if I was very changed. I studied my new beard, and wondered if it looked, maybe, silly. What would John think of me now? And what would I think of him? A decade is a long time. For some people. Others just pick up where they left off without missing a beat. Bobby and his friends were like that. I wasn't so sure about me.

I wondered what my expectations were. Did I think that John would look the same and still be in love with me? Or had he forgotten me completely until my phone call jogged his memory? Did I think that he might look old and fat and sweaty? Did I wonder if I could safely lunch with John without going gaga—again? Maybe all of the above.

We met at noon at Jacob Wirth, that fun old tin-ceilinged brewhouse just a few blocks from the theater. John looked terrific in tight jeans and a red sweater. Red always was his color. He looked tanned, and rested, and perfectly at home. But then he had always looked tanned, and rested, and perfectly at home. He gave me a fierce hug, and I was thrilled to see him again.

We got a table. "So, Bobby's doing the new show at the Charles," John said. "I have tickets for opening night! I'm so glad you decided to come with him. I hoped maybe you would. How long can you stay?"

"Only until the end of the week," I said. "I'm teaching on Monday, and I have a deadline for a magazine article, so I shouldn't have left New York in the first place."

"But I'm glad you did. What would you like to eat?" I decided on a lobster. It's hard for me to consider anything else when I'm in New England. John ordered the *wurst* platter, the other specialty of the house. Two tall drafts, and we were all set.

"I like the beard," John said. "Very distinguished."

"I'm glad you think so," I said. "I wasn't going for distinguished, exactly, but maybe for something a little more—adult."

"Absolutely." John said. "You could pass for at least twenty-three!"

I wasn't so sure about *my* looks, but it seemed to me that John had grown even more handsome in his thirties. His Iberian coloring and his fine features had settled into a more natural whole than before. His dark eyes sparkled just as they did in the old days, and when he flashed his grin at me, I melted. Just as I did in the old days.

"So, what's happening in your life?" I asked.

"The usual, mostly," he answered. "Conservation projects will keep us all busy for decades to come, unfortunately. The oceans are still getting

145

dirtier, and a lot of rivers are dead. But we have tools, and we're still plugging away. We take on polluters every day. Oyster farmers are doing a good job of keeping things clean. And the lobster populations are holding up pretty well, even as fish become scarcer."

"I admire your dedication," I said. "I never had that kind of courage."

"I think you'd be surprised to see what you have. Courage is there, when you need it." I wondered if that observation really applied to me.

"What about your love life?" I dared to ask. It just tumbled out of my mouth, even though I didn't really want to hear the answer.

"Zip, right now," he said.

"A fine catch like you, how can that be?" I asked.

"Well, I was only caught once, and then I was thrown back. But that was a long time ago," John said. "I have a job I love, and some great friends. They're the center of my life. And my parents, too, of course. I'll tell them I saw you. They were both very fond of you. Did you know that?"

"No, but I'm flattered to hear it. . . . Is that the truth?'

"Yes," John said.

"I remember that your dad was great looking," although, clearly, the son had eclipsed the father's beauty. "And I remember that he was very gracious when we went to the lobster pound to shop for our Fourth of July picnic. And I remember that your mom had a wonderfully even, accepting quality that I admired. And I loved seeing you two together." What I *didn't* tell John was that the afternoon he took me to his mother's greenmarket, I thought,

Any guy who has such a close relationship, I mean, a real love for his family, must be worth the risk—of falling in love.

What I *said* was, "Please tell them hello from me."

"Yes, of course. They'll be pleased to know I've seen you. You know, they hoped we'd get together. Even back then they had given up on any fantasies about a hetero match for me. They just wanted me to be happy. And they thought you might be the missing element."

"Oddly enough," I said, "I thought maybe *you* could complete *my* life."

"And yet, well. . ."

There was an awkward silence, and then I said, "Please tell me about your life."

"Mostly I work," John said, "and go to Provincetown for the occasional weekend. I've met some nice guys through the years, and I do love sex. Even safe sex. Speaking of which, I only know a few guys who got sick. Nobody really close other than a cousin's boyfriend. Boston wasn't hit as early or as hard as New York. How are you two dealing with the Epidemic?" John asked.

I had no ready answer, but I managed something lame, like, "We're being really careful."

"Good," John said. "I shouldn't have brought it up. Let's not talk about it. Sex is great—even safe sex—and even when it feels more like making *do* than making *love*. But I've never met another man who grabbed my heart. Hey, there's always tomorrow."

We sat quietly for a while, picking at our food and sipping our brews. Lobsters have a lot of parts that require attention. I became intent on the legs, tearing and munching. John rearranged his sausages and his sauerkraut and helped himself to more mustard.

Eventually, I was the one who broke the silence. "John, I've never forgotten how delightful you are, and how gorgeous you are. I've lost count of how many times I've fantasized about making love with you. It used to keep me awake at night. Still does. Sometimes. I had a dream once where you came to me in the night and lay down beside me, and then we were *one*. *Two* boys turned into *one* that was even better than either had been before, alone. It was my happiest dream."

John signaled the waiter and asked him to clear. "Coffee?" John asked.

"Sure," I said. And when the waiter had left the table, I said, "John, we have history."

John said, "But you have a husband, and a love for him that's much stronger than anything you ever felt for me. You talk about your fantasy. *My* fantasy was that my love would be enough for us both. I was prepared to do all the heavy lifting. I would gladly have carried us both if you had said yes."

I was struck dumb. No one in my life had ever seemed, so. . . vulnerable. Even when Bobby and I were falling in love, the openness felt so safe that we could speak our hearts fearlessly. But also without any real danger. And now John was showing me the other side. Eventually, I got myself together enough to say, "I didn't know."

"How could you?" John replied. "I never told you. But I'll bet you suspected."

"Perhaps I did," I said. "And perhaps that's why you've haunted my dreams for a decade."

"Two dreamers, in separate cities. Never mind. Anyway, you have a right to know, and maybe it could be healing. Just because my heart was broken, that doesn't mean that it can't mend."

"Beauty, brains, and heart. You're quite a package, John Alegria."

"You're not so bad yourself," he said.

I ached. All over. I wanted the glorious man across the table so badly, that I could have leapt over the coffee cups and done the fire dance barefoot over hot coals to reach him, and caress him, and *possess* him. There was the memory of stolen kisses, rolling around on John's brass bed in the little apartment he had made from the old stable behind his parents' Provincetown house. The memories now seemed tame, and chaste. *This* was something else entirely. This was *passion!*

"John," I said, "I could. . . . I would. . . .I have more to offer, now, than I did then. Maybe if we tried. . . .Maybe if you could give me another chance. Maybe we could . . .change things."

"Thank you for saying that," John said. "I know it wasn't easy. But the truth is that you and Bobby are sailing into your second decade together— smoothly, I think, but correct me if I'm wrong—and nothing is going to change that. I wanted *us* to have that. But we don't."

"What if. . ."

"No," John said.

"But, I don't want to lose you," I said.

"We lost each other a decade ago," he said.

"You make it sound so final."

"And? That feels. . .?" he asked.

"If feels like I'm missing some vital organ," I said.

"Welcome to the club."

John and I pretended to finish our coffee, and sat quietly for a minute or two. And then he said, "So, how about lunch whenever you're in Boston? I think I can just about handle that."

"It's a deal," I said. And then we split the check and headed out into the early autumn sunshine. We said our good-byes, and I clung to John a little longer than was seemly. He gave me a very nice kiss, and then he was off, back to work. I watched him go, until he had turned a corner. I felt numb. Nothing seemed real but John's kiss, John's scent, John's eyes, John's body, John's embrace. And he was gone.

I walked back into Jacob Wirth, sat on a stool at the bar, and ordered a double vodka on-the-rocks. It took the edge off. A half hour later, when I walked to the theater and sat in the back of the house to watch the end of the rehearsal, I felt very much like myself. Not my *entire* self, exactly, but close enough.

On stage, the very talented mezzo sang, "In the still of the night," and it washed over me: Cole Porter's genius for translating obsession into words and melody. Ah, yes, obsession. I understood it, perhaps even for the first time. But when the rehearsal was over, I greeted Bobby with an open heart, and we went ahead with our evening routine as if nothing had happened.

"How's John?" Bobby asked, as we walked to the T, just the two of us that evening.

"He's good. He looks terrific, and his work seems to agree with him. It was fun. He has tickets for opening night."

"That's great! Tell him to come backstage after the show. I'm so glad I'll get to see him this trip. He's a charmer. Of all the guys we met that summer in P'town, I always liked him best."

"I'll call him tomorrow and tell him to be sure to go backstage," I said.

"Is John still single?" Bobby asked.

"Yes, I think he is. Oddly enough."

"Some people are more—adaptable than others. Maybe he never found the right man."

"Maybe," I said.

"Or maybe he found the right man but couldn't have him."

"Maybe," I said. *Fuck!* I thought. *Bobby doesn't miss much. Do we really have to go into this? Do we have to dig up bodies with scarcely any breath left in them? No, that's not the truth. These bodies are very much alive. But couldn't I just have a pass this time?* The train arrived, we boarded, and in less than ten minutes we had reached our stop.

The tiny neighborhood restaurant was welcoming. Bobby was ravenous, after a long work day. He ordered a big plate of oysters, and the braised lamb shank. I decided on a few of his oysters and a composed salad with a little seafood and lots of vegetables—a sort of Boston *Niçoise*. We drank wine, and ate some very good food, and talked about the show. He asked me about my plans for the month, and I told him my teaching schedule and my writing deadlines. After dinner, the coffee was very good. And we even felt sufficiently celebratory to order an armagnac.

We were both feeling relaxed, well-fed, and glad to be alive. I know I was. We walked back to the apartment. As Bobby turned the key in the lock, he said, "Could we make it an early night? I'd really like to turn in soon, if you don't mind."

"If I could just brush my teeth," I said, "then I'd be all yours."

"I want you to be all mine whether you brush your teeth or not," Bobby said.

"Promise?" I asked,

"Promise," Bobby said.

Well I *did* brush my teeth, and Bobby brushed his, too, and then he crawled up the ladder to the very silly sleeping loft that I was so iffy about. And then I followed him. And then we made love. And then I began to feel that wonderful sense of completion that is so different from any other. Lust is wonderful. Fascination is delightful. Desire is heavenly. Infatuation is bliss. Craving is constant. Obsession is dangerous. But love?—something else entirely.

Saturday morning, I threw my stuff back into my bags, while Bobby was drinking coffee and looking very hot in the robe I made for him. Goodbyes are always creepy, I think. I was trying for the short version, but I couldn't resist dropping to my knees and going down on that beautiful dick of his that I adored so. And then I truly had no more time to spare.

We had called for a cab to get me to the train station on time. We heard the driver honk out front. Bobby said, "I'm sorry you have to go back, Sunshine. But it was sweet of you to come with me and help me get settled in. I'll miss you this month. Try not to get too lonely. And don't forget to call me every morning. But not too early!" And I knew that I had gotten my pass. And I knew that my life was good.

Bobby was standing at the door of the apartment as I gave my bags to the driver. Just as I was about to get into the cab, Bobby called to me, "The beard looks really nice, Sunshine. I think you should keep it."

"Thanks, Sweetie. I think I will."

Chapter Sixteen

The week after I returned from Boston, I was feeling a bit blah, a little tired, a little out of sorts. I met my writing deadline—a story on low-fat fish cookery, which was not a happy topic for me. But even so, I delivered some text that I hoped would be cheery, and some solid recipes that I knew would then be at the mercy of editors—olive oil measured in quarter-teaspoons, that sort of thing. I also taught a few classes—where I was free to use olive oil in proper quantities. It was all good, but I still didn't feel quite right.

Geoff called, which I thought was very kind of him. This was maybe two months before he met Ronald, so he was still outwardly-focused, as single people tend to be. And he suggested that we meet for a little supper—two bachelors, and all. I was delighted to accept. A pasta joint on the West Side? Perfect. The two of us had never spent an evening alone together, and I wasn't quite certain about our relationship—then or now. But I was grateful for the gesture.

We met early, six-thirtyish, and settled in at a little table with a red-checked tablecloth. "Did you have that beard before? I don't think so," he said.

No, it's new," I said. "What do you think?"

"It's handsome, but don't expect me to make another pass at you," he said. "You're entirely too *manly* now."

"I'll take my chances," I said. "What should I order?"

"I'd go with the linguine with clam sauce, if I were you," Geoff said.

"Linguine it is." We also ordered an antipasto of roasted peppers, Genoa salami, and marinated artichoke hearts. Two salads and a liter of house red, and we were on our way.

When the antipasto arrived, and we dug in, Geoff asked, "Did Bobby tell you how we met?"

"Yes, you were with the Jonathan Hewes show, I think."

"Most of his guests were so unpleasant, or just self-involved, or even downright nasty. So, you can imagine my pleasure when one afternoon I greeted a handsome little man who smiled and looked right into my eyes as he thanked me for taking him to the Green Room and explaining the drill. I asked him for his phone number as soon as he came offstage."

"He said *he* asked *you*," I offered. I wasn't *certain* about the truth of that, but it felt like a generous thing to say.

"Did he? Maybe," Geoff said.

"Bobby adores you, you know," I said.

"I offered myself to him once. Did he tell you that?"

"More or less."

"So, you know he rejected me."

This felt like dangerous territory, so I proceeded with the utmost caution. I said, "Geoff, I have to tell you that when we first met, it wasn't so much that I saw you as a rival as that I knew how much Bobby loves you. And I knew that I was expected to love you, too. And I wasn't entirely certain I could do it. At first. And, of course, you didn't set out to make it easy for me."

"Have I been a troll?" Geoff asked.

"No," I answered. "I thought you were probably more gracious than I might have been in the same circumstances. But I did manage to fall in love with you despite your efforts to prevent it."

"Yes, I *was* a troll. May I apologize properly?" Geoff asked, as he sank to his knees beside my chair. Now, I'm not into scenes in public places, but Geoff's contrite posture was so genuine, that I said, "Of course." And then I put my right hand on his head and said, "Bless you, my son. Rise, Sir Geoffrey. Go forth and conjugate."

Geoff was returning to his chair as the antipasto arrived. It was adequate, if unremarkable. The pasta was not bad. The salad was crunchy and refreshing rather than being really flavorful. But I figured it was giving enough, and so I finished it. And then, to my surprise, the waiter produced a generous hunk of Reggiano Parmigiano. And that put the icing on the cake, or the dot on the heart, or whatever you care to call it. We savored the cheese, and then I felt that I had dined. We moved on to coffee and Sambuca.

"And now," Geoff said, "It's story time! You promised to tell yours."

"I did, didn't I. But, Geoff, please, not tonight. I haven't really felt like myself since I got back from Boston. Nothing I can put my finger on. Just a little tired."

157

Geoff said, "Why don't you see a doctor? You probably haven't been to a doctor in an elephant's age. Actually, I know one who is perfect for you. He's a respected internist, and a gay man, so he understands our issues. And he's very attractive. And in the interest of full disclosure, I have to tell you that he holds a controversial theory about the Epidemic: He believes that the main pathogen is tertiary syphilis, due to years of over-use of antibiotics in insufficient doses to knock it out. He believes that curing syphilis that has already passed into the brain—which is notoriously difficult to diagnose—will send HIV back into the shadow realm of opportunism where it belongs. Needless to say, some health leaders think he's a crackpot. But the *VOICE* named him Man of the Year, so he also has some solid backing. Anyway, he's a good doctor, and I think you should see him and put your mind at rest about your health."

"Thank you. That's a good idea," I said.

"Yes, but you won't do it."

"I might surprise you," I said.

"You've been surprising me since the first time we met," he said.

"Is that a good thing?" I asked.

"If you make Bobby happy, then it's a *very* good thing," Geoff said.

"In that case, perhaps we could—join forces? Around a common goal."

"No sparring?" he asked.

"No more than necessary." I said.

"I like a good battle of wits, as you know. But I also love seeing my friends happily partnered. I want to see Bobby have every grace he deserves, and if you can promise that kind of devotion, then you will also have mine."

"Promise."

◫

I listened to Geoff. Not that I always did, but this time I really listened. And the next morning I made an appointment with Dr. Stefano Foscari. His secretary, Lucy, gave me an appointment in two days, and I not only kept it, but arrived early, which was rare for me back then. I liked Lucy very much. She was exactly the sort of gabby New Yorker I had expected from our phone conversation. I filled out the usual papers, and then, after a short wait, I went in to see the doctor.

I liked him even more than I liked his assistant. Steve Foscari was maybe forty, and handsome in a quiet sort of way. His manner was as low-key as his looks, and I felt instantly comfortable. He asked me the usual questions about my health, and I told him that I just felt a little run-down. I removed my shirt and sat on the examination chair. He took my blood pressure and temperature, and looked into my ears. He checked my throat. He thumped my chest and back, I think. I'm sure that's what doctors used to do back when they were hands-on.

Dr. Foscari listened to my heart and lungs. The gentle and expert way he handled his stethoscope was reassuring, to say the least. I took every deep breath—in and out—very seriously. I would have gladly followed any instruction to the letter. When he asked me to stand and drop my jeans and briefs, I was happy to comply. Dr. Foscari checked me for hernia. His hands were so warm that I would have welcomed extra rounds of coughs and head-turns, just to be certain. But once on each side was all he required.

Then he turned me around and had me bend over, elbows on the examining chair, while he put lubricant on his gloved hand. I was used to prostate exams, but I always dreaded them because they seemed so aggressive and perfunctory. Not this one, as it happened. Dr. Foscari entered very gently and almost before I sensed the intrusion he had sized up my prostate—carefully and from all angles—and withdrawn his finger. I hoped that maybe there was something more for him to do up there. No such luck.

When I had wiped the lubricant off my ass and dressed, I joined Dr. Foscari at his desk. "You seem to be in good health," he said. "Your vitals are perfectly normal. I would suggest that you eat well—which I suspect you already do—and get enough sleep—which I suspect you don't. You should probably take a good multivitamin, and some extra C. And you should also drink less. And stop smoking, of course."

Of course.

"Also, I think you should take a B12 supplement for a while. I could give you a B12 injection right now, if you like. Most people get a lift from it."

"Sure," I said. I was more than happy to drop my pants and bend over, again. Dr. Foscari's technique was flawless, again.

"See how you feel in a week or two," Dr. Foscari suggested. "If you're not one hundred percent, then come back in and we'll do some blood work."

I thanked him, and then, as I was shaking his hand, I asked, "Would you come to dinner some time, maybe you and Geoff? I know Bobby would love to meet you."

"Oh, thank you," he said. "I don't get out much these days, but that sounds very nice."

"Bobby will be back in town in two weeks. I'll call to set a date."

"Thank you," he said.

"My pleasure. And thank *you*." As I headed home, I began to feel the old spring in my step. Was it the B12 injection? Or the encouraging diagnosis? Or did it have something to do with the handsome man who had just accepted my dinner invitation? Perhaps it was all three.

📖

Bobby was pleased that I invited Steve Foscari for dinner. I checked with Geoff to find his availability, and then called the doctor. "How about next Wednesday?" I asked. "Since it's a school night, we'll be sure not to keep you out too late. 7:00?"

"7:00 it is. Thanks again."

So, things were going smoothly. I decided to put together a menu that felt rustic and just right for fall: tagliatelle with wild mushrooms; little roasted game hens stuffed with garlic, pancetta, and Swiss chard; a salad of pears and roquefort; and some imported muscat grapes afterward.

On Wednesday, I went into host mode and got things ready for our guests. Bobby helped. Dinner came together without a hitch. We were getting better at it all the time. It's always fun to look forward to good company, but that day I was also enjoying a little flutter around the heart in anticipation of seeing the good doctor again. Was it a crush? No, nothing that specific. Well, maybe.

Geoff arrived on time; Steve, about fifteen minutes later. He brought some little cookies from Caffe Roma. I thought that was a very nice gesture. And they would be perfect on our table with the grapes after dinner. Steve also made a point of greeting Scooter. Hosts always appreciate that kind of attention to their pets, of course, but Steve just fell into an easy, effortless, let-me-pet-the-dog thing that was very simple. And Scooter—always a good judge of character—approved.

We had drinks and getting-to-know-you chat, and then headed to table. Dinner was delicious, and everyone seemed to enjoy it. *Steve has a good appetite*, I noted. All was well. Over coffee and post-prandial drinks, Geoff said to Steve, "You know, Bobby was in movies when he was a kid."

"So you said. I wonder how many of them I've seen. When I was young, I hated my suburban, cookie-cutter life so much that the Late Show was the only thing that saved me," Steve said.

Geoff said, "He played a lot of war orphans and assorted other unfortunates. You might remember *The Best of Times, Leticia, This Life of Ours, Voyage to Lisbon. . .*"

Steve turned to Bobby. "You were in *Voyage to Lisbon*? The cabin boy? I can't believe this! I was maybe fourteen the first time I saw it, and when you were shot by the Nazis, I started to cry uncontrollably. I thought, *If I could just heal that beautiful boy, then my life would be worthwhile*. And I decided then and there to become a doctor."

Bobby was flattered, of course. Geoff thought it was great fun. Steve was still in shock. My reaction was a bit different:

Shit! I thought. *How is this even possible? This is supposed to be my little flirtation, and I might as well not even be here. I could strip down, stick a flag up my ass, and whistle **Dixie**, and I'd still be invisible.* But of course, I was also a host, so I had to pretend it was perfectly natural that my new flame had been carrying a torch for Bobby for his entire adult life. Longer. It took all my acting skills to pull that one off.

As promised, the evening broke up rather early, around 11:00. Geoff and Steve were both effusive with their praise for the dinner, and with their gratitude. We said our good-nights—Scooter too—and Geoff and Steve left together. Bobby straightened up a bit while I took Scooter for a quick walk. And then we all headed for the bedroom.

"Sorry to steal your thunder, Sunshine," Bobby said as we got ready for bed.

"Don't be silly," I answered, almost convincingly.

"He's very attractive," Bobby said.

"Yes, very," I said.

And then Bobby reached for me, and embraced me, and gave me a very big kiss. And it reminded me of why I had spent the last eleven years with him. When we turned out the lights, I was ready for a quiet night.

My brain had other ideas, apparently. Visions of Nazis and their helpless victims played on that screen in the middle of my head where unrest always seems to show up just when I think that *rest* is what I most need. Sometimes I was the victim, and sometimes Bobby was the victim, and sometimes I was the perpetrator.

I had worn a military uniform—quite well-tailored, mind you—on stage once in my student days. I looked good in it. Everyone said so. I *felt* good in it. Robert Taylor? Well, not quite. But it was exciting because I was newly very lean for the first time in my life. And, of course, the theatrical army in its theatrical country had nothing to do with Vietnam. Yeah, sure! Like anything in the '60s and early '70s had nothing to do with Vietnam!

That November night, in 1986, I tried very hard to make my peace with all of it. I wanted nothing but relief from the movies that were playing in my head. It felt like hours. Maybe it was only minutes. But finally, the projector went dark and the residue of the day melted into a mercifully quiet sleep.

Chapter Seventeen

Mary was red as a beet on opening night of the new show she and Bobby were performing at a small theatre on West 42nd Street. Her temperature was at least 103°. But she went on, and she managed to croak her way through the show. And since her fans came expecting a performance, more than pretty singing, she pulled it off.

Bobby came down with the same fever the next week. No shock, there. Bed rest, codeine cough syrup, and waiting it out—that was the only real path to follow. He, too, was able to perform. Just. But the evening show took all his strength, and then it was straight home to bed. I pampered him as much as possible, but there really was nothing much I could do, besides feeding him and making sure he stayed warm.

Thanksgiving was coming up, and we had reservations for an afternoon meal at a delightful restaurant in the fashion district that had a wonderful chef. Jorge Gonzalez Alvarez was a young Peruvian who had come to New York and created quite a stir introducing—almost singlehandedly—tapas! The tapas bar at the Showroom was so inviting, with lavish displays of cured meats and roasted and pickled vegetables glistening in their olive oil baths. There were platters of sautéed shrimp and grilled sardines and anchovies. Jorge also made the thickest *tortilla* (potato omelet) I've ever seen.

One of the owners of the Showroom had also produced a show of Mary and Bobby's, so we got to hang out there now and then. Not only did Jorge's kitchen turn out wonderful food, but he was such a charming little guy, so adorable, and so friendly, that I found him irresistible. Three years later he was dead. But that Thanksgiving, 1986, Jorge was very much alive, and we were excited about having our holiday dinner with him. The Festival of the Birds, he called it. So there were treats for everyone, even turkey-phobes.

Around noon, Bobby said, "I'm sorry to do this to you, Sunshine, but there's no way I can go out this afternoon. I need to spend every possible minute under the covers, or I'll never get through the show tonight."

"Of course, Darling," I said. What else could I say? "Don't worry about a thing. Bundle up, and watch your soaps. Or take a nap, and I'll feed you later."

"Thank you, Sunshine. I'll make it up to you."

"Just feel better. That's all that matters," I said.

I sprang into action, first canceling our reservation, of course. The Korean greengrocer/fish market on 2nd Avenue was open, so I dashed over and grabbed a chicken (they had a tiny meat case), some sweet potatoes, broccoli, cranberries, oranges, a loaf of bread, that sort of thing. I already had most of the other staples on hand. And then I proceeded to assemble a complete Thanksgiving feast in an hour and a half.

It looked good, it smelled good, and it tasted pretty good, too. Bobby was thankful, indeed, that he didn't have to go out. And I was thankful that I could pull it off. So, in the scheme of things, it was one of our better holidays together.

📖

A few days later, I developed a fever of my own. I shouldn't have been surprised, but I was, actually. I told myself that it shouldn't be happening, that I had never been sick a day in my life. Which was largely true. Depending upon one's perspective. But it seemed to me that Mary and Bobby snapped back faster, while I was still feeling like shit a week later.

As soon as I could bear the thought of getting dressed and leaving the house—and even before the fever had completely broken—I went to see Dr. Foscari. "I can give you some codeine cough syrup, which may make you feel a little better. But mostly I want to do some blood work, so we can get to the bottom of this. We can draw blood now, and the lab picks up in about an hour. That way the samples will be fresh, and we'll get good readings. Is that okay?"

"Sure," I said. He led me back to the waiting area.

"I'll have Lucy call you as soon as the results are in. It could be as long as a week. It's hard to know with labs. But we'll call, and we'll take it from there." His handshake was strong and reassuring. I decided I could think of other things to do with those nice hands of his. Lots of other things. Perhaps I was feeling better alter all. I thanked him.

Lucy took me to the little side room behind her desk, prepped me, and did the blood draw. Four

167

vials. It's always creepy having blood drawn, I think, even when it doesn't hurt, as in this case: Lucy slipped that butterfly's antenna into the inside of my elbow so expertly that I hardly noticed. And there was almost no bleeding after. "We'll call as soon as we know something," Lucy said. I thanked her, and headed home.

Did I fret and stew while waiting for the results? Not so much, really. Then, as now, I had a survival mechanism that allowed me to get on with my life. Answering the question, "What's for dinner?" can be a powerful normalizer. Mostly, I lived.

I should provide a little background on HIV tests. You may have noticed that Dr. Foscari never mentioned HIV, and that's not just because he was a disbeliever. In those days, HIV tests were not performed as routinely as they are now. There were very few places that offered them. That City building on First Avenue in the twenties was one of the few—the Fifties-Modern hi-rise that had scaffolding up around it for about thirty years. That one. Testing meant being assigned a number, giving the blood, and having to wait for notification of the results in three or four days, or up to a week.

The wait was harrowing, of course, and then came the return visit with one's receipt with the number on it. Those with a clear negative would be told just that. But those who tested positive or questionable would be scheduled for a consultation with a healthcare professional who could, presumably, advise them of their prognosis and suggest future care. How horrifying was that "Let's schedule an appointment" message?

But good doctors used testing sparingly because no one knew how safely *private* the results would be. Lives and careers could be wrecked. The best doctors would look at other, routine blood work to assess their patients' health, turning to the HIV test only when other factors were sufficiently out of whack. And that's part of the reason that Dr. Foscari never even mentioned the possibility.

📖

When I got the call from Lucy and then went back, exactly a week after the blood-draw, she greeted me as before. She said the doctor was running a little late, that he should be back from a hospital call in about a half-hour. I didn't mind. Lucy was fun to be with, and we laughed and joked about New York, friends, family, and food—all of life's essentials. It was more like an hour wait, but I was very accepting.

When the doctor returned, he went straight to his office. He called me in, a few minutes later, and asked me to sit down. There was something about being asked to sit before hearing the news that made my legs turn to jelly. But I made it into the chair without looking too stupid. And then he began: "Your blood work is not healthy. Here's a report, and I've circled all the numbers that are not just outside the normal range but really cause for concern." My head began to swim. I didn't know an AST from a PSD from a Creatinine or a Shmeatinine, for that matter. I hope I'm more health-savvy now, but in 1986, I was nowhere near.

"Here's what I suggest: I want to repeat the tests, today, now that you're almost a week past that fever and feeling better. And if the numbers turn out the same, then we can talk about my treatment. I don't want you to feel frightened about it. It's not that complicated. It's better performed in a hospital, but you can do it at home if you have a little help. I'm sure Bobby could help you with it. The most important part is an intravenous antibiotic program that lasts for three days. It has helped a lot of people, and you might be one of them. But first, let's get some more information."

My first thought? How do I tell Bobby? My next thought? I don't regret a single ounce of caviar I ever bought that I couldn't afford.

Lucy did the blood draw—expertly, as before. I somnambulated myself home, as before, obsessed with the situation and not really grasping the reality of it. On my way, New York City seemed determined to show me her dark side: rats scurried about on the subway tracks; scrofulous-looking bag people lurked on the benches in the station in the sickly greenish light or sprawled themselves out on subway seats; rambunctious teen-agers laughed much too loudly, as they will do when they have been released from the prison of the school day; and other, less wholesome youths seemed to dart about furtively, leaving me to guess if there would be an altercation, if knives would be drawn, if blood would be let—maybe even mine. Was there some real menace to fear? Or, was I, perhaps, just looking at the face of fear itself?

📖

When I got home, I would have put off telling Bobby as long as possible. But of course he asked me, as soon as I walked in, "So, what did Steve say?"

I sort of hemmed and hawed and couldn't quite get to the point. Bobby came to me, hugged me very gently, and said, "It's okay, Sunshine, whatever it is."

"We won't know until today's blood work comes back, but he thinks I may be sick." There, I said it. Out loud. And I was perhaps more shocked than Bobby was.

"So, then we'll wait for the lab results. And whatever happens, we'll face it together," he said.

"Thank you, Darling. I love you."

Chapter Eighteen

Bobby and I were both big fans of Christmas.
It had always provided a sense of wonder and
warmth that was less available the rest of the year.
And we had some delightful Christmases together,
including our first one, in DC. A live tree, from a
nursery somewhere nearby in Virginia, and all
those ornaments from a delightful shop in
Georgetown that I was never able to find again.
They didn't really have pop-ups in those days, so I
don't think it was something that just surfaced that
season, like Brigadoon. But the ornaments from
that phantom shop—glass birds with feathery tails,
springy tinsel icicles, a whole band of angels (musical angels, that is) with the look of ivory—formed
the core of our tree-trimming collection.

And we added on, over the years: Christmas
"cookies" from Spain, molded and decorated in colored clay; crystal stars from a giant Christmas shop
in Bethlehem—Pennsylvania; shiny little horns and
other musical instruments from Harrod's in Lon-
don; and stuffed lions, lambs, and angels with
sparkly trim from various shops in New York City.

This year, Christmas 1986, we were trying our
best to get into the spirit. I bought a tiny tree, and
we set it up—very carefully, of course, with lots of
padding and water-proofing—on top of the piano.
We put some Christmas albums on the stereo—

Johnny Mathis, Jack Jones, Roberta Peters, the Vienna Choir Boys, eclectic indeed. We got out the ornaments. And we opened Mother's package. She was good about mailing early, and it was always fun to dig into the brown paper and twine to see what awaited.

In addition to the packages to put under the tree—shirts that might not be quite to our taste, often—she would send a little tree ornament, or a rubber lizard, or maybe one of those little whirly toys that spins and flashes colored lights and sparks when you pump the little thumb-activated plunger. Scooter hated things like that. Or it might be a branch cut from a cotton bush with the puffy white fleece spilling from sharp, split bolls, ready to pick. Mother usually included at least one such Southern thing. Lest I forget. One year she sent a set of flannel bedsheets with little snowmen on them. We were happy to put them on our Christmas bed.

Scooter was delighted with the unaccustomed disorder in the room, and he quickly staked out a large piece of wrapping paper, dragged it to a corner, and settled in for a good chew. I decided it might not make for a healthy lunch, so I substituted a rawhide chewy. Scooter was disappointed, but resigned. This year's package included a model train set. Well, Bobby and I laughed and laughed. It seemed so silly, and yet delightful. It was a simple set—only a few cars and just enough track to organize a choice of two layouts—oval, or figure-eight. But it ran, and it made some choo-choo noises, and the engine car even emitted little puffs of smoke. I was beguiled, I must admit. I didn't even know that I had always wanted a model train set until my mother dipped into her reserves of whimsy (that I also didn't know much about, really) and sent her adult son (so much for adult) the perfect gift for an adolescent boy.

In no time at all, I had the track set up on the carpet under the piano—the oval layout, so that we could put gifts in the middle—and the apartment began to feel more like the Christmas House we intended to construct. I switched on the train and sent it for a few laps around the track. Scooter dropped his chewy and dashed over to investigate. I had to grab him to keep him from attacking the intruder. But he quickly made his peace with the strange new fixture, and scarcely lifted an eyebrow over it for the rest of the season.

Bobby and I finished trimming the tree and set out the porcelain boxes—the lamb that opened to reveal Fa La La La La inside was my favorite. We put jingle bells on the door handles. We hung a wreath over the kitchen door. Yes, things were taking shape.

We had decided to have a few friends—what was left of them—to dinner on Christmas Eve. It seemed the best way to celebrate, and then we would have all of Christmas Day to ourselves. Was I thinking, *This might be our last Christmas together*? No, but the thought was hiding out somewhere in my brain, half formed. Mostly I ignored it and got on with planning. It's good to be busy.

Geoff was coming, with his new friend Ronald, whom I already told you about. We were excited to be meeting him. Bobby's old friend Rachel was coming with *her* new friend Jessica. So it would be an evening of old friends and new friends: a perfect holiday mix. And three or four others promised to

stop by for drinks on their way to other engagements.

I loved working on the menu. Holiday feasts are
such fun to plan. Caution and sensibleness go
right out the window as luxury and excess take
their places. I even ordered a goose. I decided to
start with a golden squash purée soup flavored with
a little pancetta and finished with *crème fraîche* and
snipped chives. I knew I wanted to roast some potatoes in the goose fat. That was a no-brainer. And
I decided to add a bright, fresh vegetable medley of
French green beans, julienne of carrot, and tiny
cauliflower florets. And because I couldn't be certain of the weight of the goose they would send
me—and therefore its yield—I planned to have plen-
ty of meaty things on hand, including a selection of
charcuterie—country pâté, sliced prosciutto, and a
lovely aged salami studded with peppercorns. Yes,
the meats as our hors-d'oeuvre, with good crusty
bread for those who wanted it, and then the soup
as our entry into dinner proper. After the goose
and vegetables, a salad, and then a pumpkin cake
flavored with lots of sweet spice and crystallized
ginger. And then two triple-crème cheeses. And, of
course, Stilton and port and cream crackers.

As the day grew closer, I gathered ingredients
and ordered wine and spirits. Yes, we would be
ready for Christmas, ready for anything, actually.
December 24 fell on a Wednesday that year, so it
felt like a holiday gift, a chance to stretch the celebration all the way through the weekend without
feeling too guilty about idleness. Were we in a holiday humor? More or less. Vodka helped. On
Wednesday, I went on kitchen auto-pilot while Bob-

by fluffed and polished and prepared the living room for our guests.

The first of them were stopping in about 5:00. We were ready. Bobby greeted the new arrivals while I quieted Scooter. Once a few more people arrived he would become a party animal, but that first doorbell always set him off. Bobby took coats and ushered our friends into the living room. He started their drinks.

When the phone rang, I was busy arranging rich nibbles on trays. So I nearly left the call for the answering machine. But it occurred to me that a Christmas Eve phone call would most likely have some importance to it. Not a time for sales calls, or dunning calls either, for that matter. I answered.

"Hi, It's Steve Foscari," said the voice on the other end.

"Hi, Doc. Merry Christmas!" I said.

"Actually, that's why I'm calling. I have a Christmas gift for you," he said.

"I'm not following."

"Your last blood work came back today, and it's perfectly normal. It seems the dangerous numbers from before were caused by that fever you had. And now that you're past it, you don't need my treatment. So, enjoy your holidays," he said.

"Many thanks, Doc. This call means a lot. God bless you!"

"I'll take all the blessings I can get," he said.

I hung up the phone and floated to the living room, where Bobby was pouring a drink. "Could I borrow you for a minute?" I asked.

"Of course," he answered, and followed me to the bedroom.

I closed the door behind us, and said, "That was Dr. Foscari on the phone. He says I don't need his treatment. He says my last blood work is perfectly normal. He also says, 'Merry Christmas!' "

Bobby grabbed me and hugged me with all his might, which was considerable under extreme circumstances. "This is the best Christmas gift ever," he said. "Look, Sunshine, I don't know why we've been spared. But I think we must be very good to each other. So many don't get to have a future these days, and now it looks like we do. I'll try to be kinder. I'll try to be better."

"Just be *mine*," I said. And then we both laughed, realizing that we had dodged a bullet.

And then Bobby said, "Oh, shit! We have guests!" And so we did. And then the Christmas festivities *really* began.

The End

Afterword

If you think my story has a whole lot of middle-class white boys in it, then you're right. They were hard-hit. I didn't know the others who were dying at the time, the hemophiliacs and intravenous drug users and sex workers—or the Haitians or Africans, for that matter. Dr. Mathilde Krim saw it. Her team had figured out for certain by the very beginning of 1982, she said, that HIV is infectious, blood-borne, and therefore also transmitted through sex.

Even with her leadership and activism, the political and medical establishments had little interest in supporting efforts toward treatment and prevention. It wasn't until middle-class, *straight* white people started getting sick, too, that any general alarm was sounded. Everyone else was expendable.

In the beginning, there was Dr. Krim, joined by a few other scientists. And then the gay boys had to get together and figure out how to become activists. And without the support of activist lesbians— their only other allies, really—there might never have been a movement. Anything we have today in the way of AIDS treatment and prevention only exists because of the courage of those early warriors.

The famous names, of course, are ACT UP and Larry Kramer. There was a big handful of others in that league. When I think of activism, I always think first of Ann Northrup and Andy Humm. It's partly because I've known them both for years and consider them friends, but it's mostly that they were both on the front lines from early on. They both attended Dr. Krim's strategy salons, for instance, and spoke out with full-throated voices for research, treatment, and equality. And they still do, more than three decades later. I still turn to them each week at Gay USA to get my news. And they help me see how world events impact my life.

This book is not about activism, of course, but about love, and people, and loss. Some of my characters are pulled from the days of my life. And some of them are products of my overactive brain. But all of them are so dear to my heart—the real ones and the imaginary ones who have become just as real to me—that I feel a transformation in the way I live today. I suggested at the end of Chapter Thirteen that grief had to be put on hold in the '80s. I'm not the only one who had to just put it all away and get on with the business of life. Like my narrator.

I had coffee recently with a gym acquaintance who is a generation younger than I am. I was telling him about Volume II, *LOVE AND THE EPIDEMIC*. He mentioned, in passing, that he and his friends came of age in the AIDS era, that they never experienced the freedom of an earlier time. Of course, I suggested that he read Volume I, *YOU'RE SURE TO FALL IN LOVE,* if he wants to know more about the 1970s.

But what I remember most about our conversation is that he asked me if I lost many friends in the '80s. I started with my automatic answer: "I never had to watch a partner or a best friend sicken and die." Well, that's the truth, but it's less than half of the story. And as we chatted, I was bombarded with memories of wonderful men who were felled by the Epidemic.

Friends, acquaintances, colleagues, leaders, creatives in all fields. My dog groomer died, for God's sake. And my dog—who adored him—was never quite the same: For at least the next year, on our walks, he never failed to pull me over toward the front door of Gregory's little shop in the hope of stopping for a visit. I can't say which of us was more disappointed that Gregory was no longer there.

I can't even be certain how many men who sat at my dinner table were no longer around in the 1990s. The loss was unthinkable. And perhaps I unthought a lot of it. I had a keen mechanism, back then, for distancing myself from my feelings. That distancing mechanism served me well in those years, and I was able to write books and teach classes and just get on with it.

And still I knew, back then, somewhere in my brain, that I had absolutely no idea what I was feeling half of the time. Hmm, feeling. *Strong* feeling. But what is it? Could this be anger? Could this be guilt? Could this be grief? Could this be outrage? I often had no fucking idea. That didn't start in the '80s, of course. It came from childhood. How many of us stuffed and stuffed and tried to be cheerful little soldiers in the wars?

But I've lost that buffer, and I wouldn't choose to have it back. It occurred to me that writing this book has been an act of remedial grief. I spent a lot of years avoiding the fortress that stored my sorrow and loss. The walls were thick, and the battlements were high. I was protected. And then the walls came tumbling down. And I no longer have the luxury of that protection from the necessity of grieving. I have been forced to start the process. And the most vivid result is that now I share my life with ghosts. And I must say, I find them excellent company.

This is a first edition from
Audacity Books
Please visit us on the web at
www.audacitybooks.com
For information, please send your request to
info@audacitybooks.com.

LOVE AND THE EPIDEMIC, set in New York City in the mid-'80s is Volume II of Bruce K Beck's **Love Trilogy.** Look for Volume I, *YOU'RE SURE TO FALL IN LOVE*, set in Provincetown, MA, in the summer of 1976. Coming soon is Volume III, *AND LOVE ENDURES*, set in the early 1990s. For updates, please subscribe at www.audacitybooks.com.

Many thanks to Sonya Teclai, Social Media Director at Audacity Books, for her support throughout the project. Particular thanks to Kathie DeNobriga, Lukas Hassel, and Denise Paradiso for their generous wisdom. And to Richard Kutner for his classy edits. Tim Barber of Dissect Designs (www.dissectdesigns.com) signed on as a cover designer, and became a friend. You're sure to fall in love, indeed. This journey would not have been possible without the example and the teaching of Joanna Penn at www.thecreativepenn.com. I am delighted, Joanna, to add this volume to your long list of books you have enabled. No doubt you will hit your one million mark any day now!

Readers are invited to listen to the
YOU'RE SURE TO FALL IN LOVE Playlist at
www.youresuretofallinlove.com

Bruce K Beck is both a writer and an accomplished chef. Before turning to fiction, he authored ***PRODUCE: A FRUIT AND VEGETABLE LOVERS' GUIDE***, which was called "gorgeous" by **The New York Times**, "a dazzler" by **Bon Appetit**, and "the most spectacular food book of the year" by **The Boston Globe**. His next book was ***THE OFFICIAL FULTON FISH MARKET COOKBOOK***, which was called "invaluable" by Jacques Pépin, and "a treasure" by Irene Sax of **Newsday**. And Rex Reed said, ". . .you'll love this book. It's like a movie!"